Lady Ludmilla's Accidental Letter

Sofi Laporte

Copyright © 2022 by Alice Lapuerta.

http://www.sofilaporte.com

sofi@sofilaporte.com

c/o Block Services
Stuttgarter Str. 106
70736 Fellbach, Germany

Editor: Caroline Barnhill
Cover Art: Victoria Cooper

ISBN: 978-3-9505190-5-1

❀ Created with Vellum

Chapter One

No one knew that Lady Ludmilla Marie Windmere, spinster extraordinaire, had a delicious secret.

Her best friend was someone with whom she corresponded through letters.

And he was a *man*.

Lu had no doubt he was a gentleman, but she could not know for sure, for she'd never met him, nor did she know his full name. What's more, she did not *want* to know his full name. Because then, she'd have to reveal *her* full name, and that she wouldn't do. For that would mean the end of their correspondence.

Every respectable lady knew that it was excessively indecorous for a lady to maintain a correspondence with a man with whom she was not acquainted.

It was not proper.

It was not seemly.

It was simply not *done*.

Lady Ludmilla, the epitome of propriety and good conduct, did not care a whit.

She tore the letters open before she reached her room, perused them on the stairs and in the hallway, laughing out loud. Then she clasped a hand over her mouth, because laughing out loud was frowned upon in Great Aunt Mildred's house in Bath. As was rushing up the stairs. One had to tread quietly, preferably on tiptoes, avoiding the creaky upper stair, never slam a door, never raise one's voice, and never, heaven forbid, laugh. Because all these things exacerbated Mildred's migraine. And one did not, under any circumstances, ever, want to do that.

Lu kept those letters secret from her aunt. She'd trained Hicks, the butler, to deliver the missives to her directly, discreetly, and whenever Great Aunt Mildred was not around.

On a rare occasion, she'd press the letter to her chest, with an odd smile on her lips and a star in her eyes. Those letters, witty, infinitely charming, understanding, and kind, were the only thing that made her life with her aunt bearable. Her epistolary friendship added colour and spice to her existence. She lived for those letters.

IT HAD STARTED WITH A MISUNDERSTANDING.

Three years ago, she'd written a letter to a former childhood friend, Miss Susan Millsbury, who lived in Bruton Street, London, and who, she'd learned, had recently married. Lu had written a letter of congratulations and went off a tangent on a particular childhood memory that she and Susan shared. It involved a monkey. She requested Susan to reply to her new abode in Bath. And because Susan was an old childhood friend of hers, she merely signed her letters with a very informal "Lu".

After two weeks, someone else replied with pretty penmanship. It was addressed to Madam "Lu" with apostrophes. Hicks was intelligent enough to decipher that it must be addressed to Lady Ludmilla and presented her the letter on a silver tablet at breakfast one morning.

Lu took it, turned it over, inspected the seal—a simple letter 'A' wound around by an arum lily—and broke it with growing curiosity.

DEAR MADAM 'LU',

I must apologize. I accidentally opened and read your (vastly entertaining) letter that was sitting on top of my correspondence. Your friend "Susan" seems to have been the prior tenant of this house. There is no Susan living here now.

Respectfully yours,

(illegible scribble that read like "Addy")

P.S. I am all agog to learn what happened to the escaped monkey after you rescued it from the tree. The suspense is killing me. Pray relieve me from that suspense. Is the monkey still living with you? I also want to have a monkey!

Lu WAS in the process of biting into a brioche when she read the missive. She choked on a laugh, and nearly sprayed crumbs all over the table. Her aunt looked up with such a woeful look of suffering that Lu's laughter died on her lips instantly.

"I apologise, Aunt. A crumb went down the wrong way."

"My great uncle Bartholomew died because a crumb went down the wrong way. It got lodged in his airpipe and completely clogged it shut. Suffocated. Asphyxiated. Expired. Breathed his last." She sighed and stared with tragic eyes at the ceiling.

"But Aunt, he can't have breathed his last if he suffocated simultaneously," the ever-reasonable Lu pointed out.

"My dear Ludmilla. This is beside the point. The point is that he died a most horrific death because he laughed while eating. At least he did not die of the black pox, like his sister."

"How terrible." Lu set down her butter knife, having lost all appetite to finish her breakfast. She squinted with longing at her letter on her lap.

"Your eyes must be getting bad, Ludmilla," her aunt observed. "Do you need to see an oculist?"

"No, Aunt, I merely forgot to put on my glasses."

"Don't forget to take some of Dr Rothely's Famous Purging Elixir to be on the safe side."

"How would ingesting Dr Rothely's Elixir help a weak eye?" Lu couldn't help but ask.

"Put a drop of it in your eye, child, for good measure. There." She waved Ludmilla away. "I can feel my migraine returning. I shall lie down." Lu did not point out that her aunt had just gotten up. Lu excused herself, returned to her room, sat by the desk, and immediately proceeded to reply.

DEAR MISS ADDY,

Oh no! We certainly can't have you killed, not over something as trivial as a monkey. I had no idea my friend Susan no longer lives there. She has been remiss in informing me that her lease was up, and she must have moved back to York. The monkey, which seems to have escaped from a traveling troupe of actors, was most peculiarly attached to me, particularly after I proceeded to feed it with sugar plums. I posted an announcement in The Times, and after three days, the Jollyphus troupe claimed her. It was most difficult shifting her attachment from me back to her original owner. She climbed up my chintz curtains and refused to come down. It took them three hours and a plate full of sugar plums to coax her down. The poor thing was violently sick on my father's Persian carpet afterwards. The lesson learned was not to take home strange animals, and not to feed them sugar plums, ever. I'd named her Renalda, poor thing.

Lady Lu–

Lu normally signed her letters formally as "Lady Ludmilla Windmere" and sealed them with a pretty wax seal. However, because her aunt's maid barged into her room, interrupting her, requesting that she go see her aunt most urgently, for she was suffering the greatest pains, requesting a vial of Dr Graham's Tonic, which Lu kept in her drawer, she broke off her signature. On her way to her aunt's room, she pressed the missive into Hicks's hands and told him to post it.

"Who do I address it to, Madam?"

"A Miss Addy, in Bruton Street, Mayfair, London."

"Ludmilla!" her aunt groaned from her room.

"I am coming, aunt!" She entered her aunt's room with the tonic.

To her surprise, Miss Addy answered promptly.

My dear Lady "Lu," (what kind of a name is that? Short for Ludwiga?)

You had me chuckling over your account of Renalda the monkey. Sugar plums? Really? Wouldn't the creature have been more amenable to apples and nuts? But what do I know of these wild creatures? Sugar plums may very well have been the thing. (I now feel an irresistible craving for sugar plums myself; after all, they are my favourite kind of sweet).

Let me guess. If you were to run across a mangled, half-starved mongrel in the street tomorrow morning, you would take it in. And feed it sugar plums. You seem to be exactly that kind of damsel.

Your Servant,

Addy (off to seek some sugar plums)

P.S. Alas, my sense of chivalry tells me that I must reveal: I am neither Miss nor Madam.

SHE SHOULD HAVE BROKEN off the communication immediately. It simply wasn't done to entertain a letter correspondence with a man, a stranger, who signed only with his given name, to boot. How unorthodox! But she simply, simply could not leave that question unanswered. If he refused to reveal his full name, then she would, as well.

DEAR MISTER 'ADDY',

I shall not tell you my name for I fairly abhor it! "Lu" is just fine. Besides, if you are not revealing your complete name, then neither shall I. And let me disillusion you right away: I am no damsel. Oh! How did you know? I did indeed rescue a mongrel off the streets the other day. It was a pitiful, small thing, more dead than alive. You do me great injustice! Of course, I did not feed it sugar plums (it turned up its nose when I offered them) but a bowl of milk (which it hurled up all over our Wilton carpet). It recovered eventually and had a tendency to chew on the sofa legs, and bark. Which, one could argue, is perfectly natural behaviour for a dog. Except his bark was so unnaturally high-pitched, it caused the inhabitants of this house to develop a migraine. So, I had to give him away. A shame, for I'd named him Coriolanus.

Lu

P.S. Did you enjoy your sugar plums? I, myself, hold no great affection towards sweets. I prefer my food to be savoury.

My dearest not-a-damsel-Luciana (*I shall call you that for the lack of a real name*):

You are not playing fair. I told you my name, and you leave me guessing yours? Coriolanus is an excellent name for a dog. My own dog is named Macbeth. He is a Bloodhound, a gentle soul, and a most loyal friend. You'd take an irresistible liking to him and feed him sugar plums...

Their exchange had been too deliciously bantering that she just could not give it up. Three years and hundreds of letters later, she was still writing to "Addy," who had become her best friend. She was rather fond of him, more than fond, excessively fond—in fact, something tugged painfully at her heart every time she thought of him, but she dared not admit that. They discussed books (Addy was astonishingly well read, almost as much as she), exhausted the topic of dogs, horses, monkeys, and other animals, and oh! Theatre. Addy had seen every single play and opera that was performed in London, and Lu, who used to love going to the theatre, was jealous.

Lu, normally shy with most people, told him every tidbit of her life. About her previous life at Whistlethorpe Park, where she'd grown up. Until her father died, and she moved in with Great Aunt Mildred in Bath. He knew all about her and that her biggest dream was to buy a cottage in the country where she could live in peace and quiet on her own, unbothered by society. The only thing she did not share with him was her name. She feared it would kill the magic. She feared that if he knew she was a

Windmere and discover who she really was—a plain spinster, a nobody with neither looks, prospects, nor particular talents aside from reading (and writing correspondence)—he'd line up with all the other men who'd looked her over, then let a mask of politeness slide over their faces before they slunk over to her more attractive relations.

She would rather die.

For alas, Lu had not inherited the famous Windmere beauty that her family was known for. Lu had the misfortune to have a large family where each member, without exception, was smashingly handsome. The men were tall, chin-dimpled, chestnut-maned, broad-chested, strapping fellows, while the women were tall, dimpled, buxom, blonde-curled, porcelain-skinned English beauties.

Except for her.

Lu was the sore stick in the pile. She was small, lithe, flat-chested, brown-eyed, and snub-nosed. If that were not enough, she had freckles. Her skin, though clear, tended to have a sallow-tinted hue because of all the browns, olives, and khakis she wore. And her straight, black hair stubbornly refused to curl. There was simply nothing to be done about it. While her vibrant sister drew all the attention every time she entered a room, Lu embodied everything contrary to the current beauty ideal.

She was invisible.

So, surrounded by beauties, it was refreshing to have this one acquaintance who neither knew—nor cared—what she looked like.

Addy liked her for her brains. Her wit. Her humour.

Addy liked her for being herself.

Addy teased her ruthlessly. She'd never been teased before. Not by a man! And she enjoyed every minute of it. He called her all sorts of variants of Lu—Lucinda, Luisa, Ludwina, Luitgard. She adored it! To date, he had not hit on her correct name. How deliciously improper it was!

Chapter Two

"Luuuuudmilla!"

Mildred's plaintive call echoed in the hallway, preceding Hicks, who entered the room with a doleful expression on his face. "Her Ladyship requires your presence, my lady."

Lu set down her quill. "So I hear. Did the migraine get worse?" She cast a quick look at the window, where the heavy dark brown brocade curtains were drawn aside to allow the daylight to flood into the drawing room. Lu's room was the only room where the sunlight was allowed in. The remaining windows in the house, from the cellar to the attic, were firmly shut and shrouded by heavy, dark curtains. For Mildred believed her headache came from the persistent sunlight and had directed the domestics to keep all curtains drawn. The result was that the atmosphere of the house resembled that of a morbid tomb. Only Lu kept drawing the curtains aside, thereby being responsible for her worsening migraines.

"No, the migraines seem to have miraculously healed."

"Oh, did they, Hicks?" Lu threw him an amused glance. "What is it this time, then?"

"Bunions, my lady." Hicks did not move a muscle in his face at the aunt's newest ailment.

"Oh dear." Lu got up. "Thank goodness it's only the bunions!"

Great Aunt Mildred had been struck by ulcers, heart disease, scrofula, scarlet fever, and the plague within the span of only a single morning. It was only with great difficulty that Lu had talked her out of calling poor Doctor Allen every time she came up with a new ailment. "Has she called the doctor yet?"

"Not yet."

"Tell Mary to bring up a basin with hot water, towels and Dr Rothely's Purging Elixir."

"The elixir, my lady?" The scepticism was clear on Hick's face.

Lu sighed. "You have to put something into the water to cure her bunions. Might as well put in several drops of the elixir. You know how she believes it to be a cure-all." Lu thought. "That is, supposing that she won't be amenable to cutting off the bunions. She will likely not acquiesce to that."

"Very likely, my lady."

Before she set off to see her aunt, she lowered her voice and asked Hicks. "Did a letter arrive?"

Hicks understood immediately. "No. But one from your sister did."

She scrunched up her face in worry. "Jessica? I hope

nothing is the matter." Jessica fairly detested writing letters. She only wrote when she wanted something, like the newest roll of chintz lace that Lu had bought but never used, or Mama's pearl necklace. Lu hadn't minded sending her the chintz, but she would never part with Mama's pearl necklace. Her mother had given it to her directly before she died, and it was the only thing she'd left of her mother. She'd quarrelled bitterly with Jessica over this, and Jessica hadn't written a line to her ever since. Lu wondered why she was writing now.

"Lady Mildred has requested to leave your letter in the drawing room. She requires you to attend to her first."

Lu frowned and went downstairs.

In the dark room, Lu discerned the shape of her great aunt, who lay reclined on the green sofa, a wet wash towel over her eyes, her naked feet propped on a pillow.

"Ludmilla, is that you?" Her voice was weak and plaintive.

"Yes, Aunt. How can I help?"

"Oh! The pain!" her aunt groaned.

To give her credit, her feet did look swollen, and the protruding bone on each side of her foot was red.

"Ella tried to massage them, but she presses too hard," her aunt complained. "I want you to do it. You have such gentle, soft fingers."

Lu pulled a face at the thought of massaging her aunt's smelly, corn-covered feet.

"Where is Ella?" Lu looked around for her abigail.

"I sent her to the apothecary for Graham James's Imperial Pills. They are said to have a purging effect. In addition to some more laudanum. We ran out of laudanum." She could have sent the footman, of course, but Mildred had a tendency to make her servants do whatever whim befell her. Once, she made Hicks unravel an entire basket of woollen scarves that she'd knitted. Then he'd had to stand in front of her for two hours holding the wool between two hands, while Ella rolled them into two balls. The entire time, Mildred had stood next to them, complaining about the colour of the wool.

Lu frowned. "You know you shouldn't take too much laudanum. I did have Mary add some of the Purging Elixir to the foot bath."

"You are a sweet girl," her aunt said weakly. "What would I do without you?"

Her aunt ingested far too much laudanum. She was dependent on it for curing every single ailment that befell her, imaginary and otherwise. After an initial burst of energy, however, it always left her listless and in low spirits.

Mary entered with the basin of warm water, and Lu helped her aunt sit up and placed her feet in it.

"Aaah." Mildred leaned back and closed her eyes.

Lu sat down, placed a towel over her lap, took one foot on it, dried it, and began to massage it gently.

Mildred groaned.

"There, there. You will feel better imminently," Lu told her in a soothing voice.

Her aunt growled in contentment and was, thankfully, for the moment quiet.

Maybe she would fall asleep, Lu hoped. She peeked at the two letters lying on the table next to her aunt. One was addressed in bold handwriting to Lady Mildred

Arbington; the other was from her sister. It was addressed to her. Lu picked it up and slipped it into her bodice.

After she'd massaged and creamed her aunt's feet, she asked, "Would you like me to read you the letter, Aunt?"

"No. Yes. I will read it later. But my eyes hurt terribly. What if I have developed an eye disease and will go blind?"

"Let me read it to you, then. So you don't overexert your eyes."

"Very well," her aunt acquiesced with a groan. "I daresay my migraine is returning."

Lu retreated to the window to draw the curtains aside.

"Must you do that?" her aunt complained as she shifted on the pillow to evade the light. "Light tends to exacerbate the pounding in my head."

"I am sorry, Aunt. But I need light to read the letter. Or do you want me to light a candle?" It was barely noontime, and the sun was shining brightly outside. "It would be a shameful waste of beeswax, however."

"Very well, pull the curtains aside a little, but make sure the sunrays don't touch my face."

Lu pulled the curtains aside and threw out a longing look into the garden. It was a bright, fresh, spring day, and if she were still living in her home at Whistlethorpe Park, she'd spend the entire morning walking through the beautiful park landscape, spend some time gardening in the rose garden, or even sit in the maze to read her correspondence, instead of being holed up inside this musty tomb. But Whistlethorpe Park was no longer her home. It hadn't been since her father, the Duke of Amberley, died, and the title and estate had been passed on to Cousin Hector, son of her father's brother, who was now the new duke. He hadn't wanted the two spinsters, as he called them, in his home, which hitherto had been theirs. So, Lu had moved in with Great Aunt Mildred in Bath, while her sister Jessica lived with Aunt Ernestina in London.

"I am not a spinster!" Jessica had been enraged at the label. "I am not yet eighteen, and I will get married soon, just you wait."

Lu had merely sighed. It may be debated that Jessica had drawn the better lot, living with Aunt Ernestina in London, the season right at their doorstep. But Lu did not mind. She hated London; she hated the season and the marriage mart. She wanted nothing to do with it.

She wished she could live in a little cottage in the country, tending to some chickens, embroidering, reading books, and writing letters to Addy.

This, or return to Whistlethorpe Park. But that was lost to her forever.

She suppressed the stab of homesickness that pierced her heart. She lifted the letter.

"It's from Aunt Ernestina," Lu read. "Dear Mildred, I hope this letter finds you well. As you know, I am sponsoring Ludmilla's sister Jessica in London for her season. It would be a great advantage to both girls if Ludmilla were to join us in London. Jessica needs company, and Ludmilla no doubt needs some polishing—" Lu swallowed.

"What are you saying? Don't mumble so," her aunt complained. "You shall have to reread the letter, for I have not understood a single word. Maybe there is something wrong with my ears? Maybe I am developing an ear infection?"

Lu sighed and reread the letter. "—polishing of her countrified manners. It would be good for her to acquire some town bronze. Besides, I am sure you agree, it is time for the girl to find a husband." Lu coughed out the latter words.

Mildred sat up, the wash towel still on her forehead. "Ludmila going to London? To get married? Oh, but how could you?"

Lu uttered a dry laugh. "I agree entirely. It is laughable. I am far too old to get married." She found Ernestina's optimism amusing. Lu was a dried-up spinster, heading towards thirty, and no man would look at her twice.

Besides, the last time she was in London, it had ended in tears, disaster, and heartbreak. Lu shuddered. She'd vowed she'd never repeat this experience. Ever.

"How could you leave me all alone when I am so unwell?" Mildred shook her head vehemently. "No, no, no, no. Emphatically no. I can't have that. You will stay here, and Ernestina will have to find another companion for Jessica. London is full of females who can fill that role. I can absolutely not dispense with you. I shall write to Ernestina immediately and tell her the idea is nonsensical."

"Very well, Aunt." Anyway, she had no friends in London. No one missed her or would even want to talk to her. The balls were all the same, she'd seen them all and felt no desire to attend again. Except Vauxhall maybe, which really was very pretty with all the fireworks lighting up the night sky. And the opera. She did miss that. The Theatre Royal in Bath had a good reputation, but the opera in Covent Garden was another world entirely. She'd adored going there every Saturday night with her father, for he'd been as much of an opera enthusiast as she. It had been so long since she'd last been to the theatre. To get away from Great Aunt Mildred and her ailments, if only for one afternoon, was tempting...Lu sighed.

But she had decided she hated London, didn't she? She was better off in Bath. Most decidedly.

"Besides, I have heard the air in London is most noxious and insalubrious. You will come down with a pulmonary ailment in no time, mark my words."

"Yes, Aunt." Lu folded the humid towel and clutched it in front of her.

Surely, surely it was better to remain in Bath.

There was nothing for her in London.

Chapter Three

Things took a surprising turn a week later.

Mildred had written a firm but emphatic 'No' on Lu's behalf. Lu told herself she was fine with it. The only twinge of conscience was Jessica.

Jessica, who'd written, rather prettily, *"I so wish you'd forgive me for having behaved as a spoiled brat. Show me that you forgive me by joining me in London. Isn't Aunt Ernestina's idea splendid? I shall so enjoy showing you the sights of London."*

Lu had been relieved and happy about Jessica's letter and spent nearly two hours crafting a suitable reply as to why she had forgiven her but still wasn't able to go to London.

She hadn't received a reply to that.

Several days later, Hicks announced, with a doleful face: "Lady Ernestina Rutherford and Lady Jessica Windmere are here."

Lu dropped her embroidery, and Mildred sat up

straight on the sofa, a washcloth still covering her eyes, when Ernestina swept into the room, followed closely by Jessica.

"Aunt! Jessica!" Lu found herself squashed against an ample bosom and was handed over to Jessica's exuberant embrace.

"Oh, Lu! Lu! I am so happy to see you!" Jessica was dressed in vibrant pink colours, with a matching bonnet. Her cheeks were rosy, and her eyes sparkled. With a pang, Lu realised her little baby sister had grown up into a beautiful young lady.

"Jessica! I had no idea you were coming!" Lu managed to say in between two squeezes.

"What is happening? I can't see anything," Mildred lamented.

"Take that cloth off your head, Mildred," Ernestina picked the washcloth off her forehead with two fingers and dropped it on the table.

Mildred blinked in astonishment. "Ernestina? Good heavens. It is you!"

Ernestina Clemens, Lady Rutherford, was not directly related to Mildred, since Mildred was Lu's mother's aunt, and Ernestina was Lu's father's sister; however, they called each other by given name since they were nearly the same age. Ernestina was, as she liked to remind people, a born Windmere and would stay one until she died.

Ernestina took Lu's chin in her hand and tilted it upwards. "We happened to be in Bath and decided to drop by. You look thin and pale, child. Are you eating enough?"

"Well, yes, Aunt."

"Hump. I can't see anything in this darkness here." She went to the windows and yanked the drapes aside. Sunshine flooded through the windows and revealed a morning room with dour oaken furniture.

"We did not expect you." Mildred squinted and lifted her hand to shield her eyes from the light.

"No, likely you did not." Ernestina pulled the fingers of her gloves off one by one. "How is your gout? Or was it dropsy? I can't recall."

"Bunions, it was," Lu muttered.

"Dropsy?" Mildred blinked, as if she'd forgotten entirely about that illness. "It is, rather, dyspepsia which plagues me. But if you come and think of it, the dropsy may still be lingering as well. Must we have all this light? It hurts my eyes."

"Fiddlesticks." Ernestina pulled the curtains even farther apart. "This place is as dark as a cave. How can you bear it? I daresay your ailments come from lying around all day doing nothing. Of course, one must fall ill when one has nothing to occupy oneself." Ernestina never minced matters.

"Really, Ernestina," Mildred replied with a sulking tone. "Not everyone has the good fortune to be in as strapping good health as you. You appear to be as healthy as a horse."

"Indeed. I can't recall when it was the last time I was ill. But no matter. We have come all the way from London to pick up Ludmilla."

"That is very kind of you, Aunt, but I believe Aunt

Mildred needs me here." Lu clasped her hands in front of her.

"I do, indeed." Mildred sniffed. "It is unfortunate you came this long way from London, but as you see, Ludmilla is much needed here."

Ernestina tusked. "To do what? Pick up the hartshorn salt for you? You have your lady's maid for that." She scrutinized Lu. "No. It is best Lu comes with us to London for this season. It is high time for her to do so. In fact, I regret that I did not insist she join us from the very beginning. The two sisters ought to be together; it will also do Jessica good to have a companion."

Jessica drew Lu aside. "We are to go to balls and such. I am to be introduced at court. Oh, do come, Lu! I wouldn't want you to miss this for the world."

Lu felt herself break out in a sweat. "But I've already had a season, and, you may have forgotten, I was not a success."

"Let us face the facts. Lu is too old to get married." The cruel words came from Mildred.

"You seem to forget, Mildred, that you yourself married rather late. How old were you again? Forty? Fifty?" Ernestina asked with a raised eyebrow.

"I was forty-two. But that isn't quite the same thing. John had courted me for a good decade before that."

"Lu is not yet thirty. So, I daresay, there is still hope for her," Ernestina said.

Lu rubbed her eyes tiredly. "Please, Aunt. I know you mean well, but Mildred is right. I am long past marriageable age. A season for me would be entirely futile, in addition to being a colossal waste of money."

"Fiddlesticks. Don't talk about money in my presence, it is vulgar. We Windmere women are not meant to be spinsters. There hasn't been a single spinster in the lineage since the beginning of time. Windmere women are married women. It is a fact. I will see you married if it's the last thing I ever do." Ernestina looked around. "Can a person have some tea in this house? Preferably something unlaced with laudanum or other tonics."

"Of course, Aunt." Lu rang the bell and wondered whether her Aunt Ernestina was suffering a tiny bit of delusions of grandeur. Windmere women were married women since the beginning of time, indeed!

After each was served a cup of tea with dry shortbread, Ernestina and Mildred continued to squabble over this.

Jessica squeezed Lu's hands. "You're the only real family I have left, you know," she murmured into Lu's ear. "Aunt Ernestina is kind and everything, but sometimes I miss company. I miss you. You're the only one who remembers what it was like when Papa and Mama were alive and we used to live at Whistlethorpe Park together. Now, Cousin Hector lives there as the new duke, and it isn't the same. Sometimes I'm a little homesick."

Lu squeezed her hands. She understood homesickness only too well.

They'd lost both parents within a short time. Jessica was right. She was the only living family member Lu had left, and Lu owed her more loyalty and allegiance than she did to Mildred.

23

But the season. The balls. The humiliation. Lu slumped. Was she to repeat all that?

On the other hand, it had been such a very long time ago. Jessica had been a child when Lu had had her first season. A lot of water had passed under the bridge since then. Surely, many things must have changed in London as well?

"I am just not sure London agrees with me." Lu stirred in her teacup slowly, took the spoon out of her cup and laid it into the saucer carefully.

"Or do you mean to say you do not know whether you agree with London? I know things haven't been easy for you in the past, and the last thing I want is to cause you pain by reliving it all. But don't you think by returning you could put aside some of those ghosts?"

Lu gave her sister a startled look. Uncanny how wise Jessica could be when she chose to set aside her spoiled pretty girl image.

"Besides, Aunt Ernestina would grant me—us—more liberty if you were to come. We could go do things, like see the tightrope walkers in Vauxhall or the circus performers. And there are many booksellers and libraries, did you know? The Temple of the Muses, for one."

This caught Lu's attention. "The Temple of the Muses? Have you been there?"

"Not yet, because Aunt doesn't care much about reading. This is my point. With you, we could go together and seek out those places. There are many more!"

Bath, of course, also had lending libraries and book-sellers aplenty, but they received their stock from

London. Lu chewed around on her lower lip thought-fully. It was terribly tempting.

"Oh, do come, Lu. Please." Jessica shook her arm. "It would mean so much to me."

"If Great Aunt doesn't need me—" Lu began before she was interrupted by Ernestina.

"Of course, she doesn't."

"Of course, I do!" Mildred exclaimed.

Lu looked helplessly from one aunt to another.

"Of course, I need you," Mildred repeated and fell back into her pillows, with an arm slung over her eyes for dramatic emphasis. "But I see I am quite overcome. It is futile to resist. Go to London, child, and amuse yourself. I shall face and conquer my illnesses on my own."

Ernestina rolled her eyes, and Jessica clapped her hands. "How splendid!"

Lu ran her tongue over her dried lips. Her fingers cramped over her embroidery. "Very well." She'd do this for Jessica.

She was to go to London.

Dear heavens.

DEAREST ADDY,

The unthinkable has happened! We are to go to London. We are to have a season. Oh, the horror!

That is, of course, my sister Jessica is to have her first season, and I am to come along in my aunt's final, desperate attempt to get me off the shelf. Alas, they insist on dragging me from my dark and dusty corner, where I am sitting rather comfortably, thank you very much. Is *there no way for me to get out of this? You know how much I <u>loathe</u> having to be social. I am fairly quaking in my shoes.*

Yours, most unhappily,

Lu

MY DEAREST QUAKING LUITPOLDINA,

The horror, indeed! I shall quake alongside you. There is nothing worse under the sun than having to face the infamous marriage mart, with its pale, husband-chasing damsels and their ambitious Mamas.

Alas! And you are to enter their ranks?

But never my Lu?

A point to think about, my dear Lu, should you decide to venture forth from your dark and dusty corner on the shelf: I would await you in the sunshine, and perhaps we could take a walk together in Hyde Park?

Let me know where you are staying, so I can call on you.

It would be a pleasure.

Always yours,

Addy

LU HADN'T REPLIED to this letter.

She'd felt something odd course through her. This letter was different. Not only because Addy had, for the first time, suggested meeting for real. There was something more. What had he meant by he'd wait for her in the sunshine if she ventured forth from her shelf? And how he'd written "my Lu". So oddly ... intimate. Something unfamiliarly hot rushed through her veins. And, how he signed. Her eyes were fixated on "Always yours". He'd never signed like that before. It'd been "Your servant" or "In friendship yours". But "Always yours" ... Lu dropped the letter, sighed, and stared with a dreamy look at an empty spot on the wallpaper.

Something had shifted.

But what?

Meet her Addy in real life? Her stomach did a triple somersault.

She sat down and wrote one letter, crumpled it up, and wrote a second one. Then a third. Soon, the floor was littered with crumpled little paper balls.

DEAR ADDY,

I am terrified. What if you are not who I think you are?—

DEAR ADDY,

How can we meet? You are a man. Judging from your letters, a man of the world. Intelligent, witty, charming, probably attractive, too. Am I right? I am a spinster with no great beauty. An unmarried lady who is starting to find herself attracted to—

DEAREST ADDY.

Oh, how lovely if we could finally meet! Shall we say Wednesday after our arrival—

LU CHEWED on the tip of her quill. She'd nearly plucked out all the feathers and would now need to buy a new one. She threw down the quill in exasperation and splattered ink all over the paper.

28

She couldn't meet Addy.

Ever.

She just couldn't. He would expect someone else entirely, and she couldn't bear to see the disappointment in his eyes when he realised who she was. A drab old spinster. With nothing, really, to offer. No wit, no beauty, nothing.

No, it was safer that he stayed her dear friend and correspondent, at a far distance only.

Lu stared sadly at the paper in front of her.

In the meantime, she would put her entire energy into helping Jessica find a suitable husband. For, if Jessica married, Lu reasoned, she might move in with her for a while. Away from Mildred. And then she could maybe find the courage to access her funds in the bank in London and buy herself a cottage in the country somewhere. With some chickens and a goat.

And she could continue to write letters to Addy as she sat on the bench in front of her hut and watched her chickens.

Lu shook her head and snorted.

What nonsense.

It was time to stop dreaming.

Maybe, it was time to stop writing to Addy altogether.

Ah, if only her heart allowed it.

Chapter Four

In the house of Bruton Street 4B, London, Mr Adam Adey pushed his coffee aside. He felt no great appetite for the eggs and bacon, either. "James. Is there a letter for me?" he asked the butler.

"No, sir."

"Check again, will you?" He drummed his fingers on the tabletop.

Viscount St Addington threw a quizzical look at his cousin and folded up his newspaper. "You seem uncommonly restless these days. Is anything the matter?"

Adam jumped up, walked up and down, sat down again. "I'm sorry, Cousin. I'm waiting for a letter. I'm somewhat nervous these days."

"I've noticed. Let me guess. A woman?" A flicker of humour passed through the viscount's eyes.

"No," Adam said. "Maybe." He swallowed painfully. "Yes."

"No? Maybe? Yes? Well, what's it to be?"

"I suppose so, yes."

31

St Addington shook his head. "Pray enlighten me, Cousin."

"I am thinking about getting married," Adam burst forth.

"Dear me! Behold me flabbergasted. You're pulling the rug from underneath my feet. You want to get shackled? In all seriousness?"

Adam pulled a hand through his hair. "One has to settle down one day, don't you think? Start a nursery and all that."

"A nursery! Good heavens." The viscount looked horrified. "Have we finally reached this point?"

Adam was defensive. "There is nothing wrong with that, is there? It's our duty after all, isn't it? Yours as well, if I might add. Except you're particularly good at evading it. I can't be quite like that. I admit I've been thinking about it for a while. With a good sort of woman. In fact, there can be nothing more delightful that life has to offer than to have one's own family with a good woman."

A look of satirical amusement crossed St Addington's face. "A good sort of woman. Therein lies the rub. Do you think such a mythical creature exists? Do you have anyone particular in mind?"

Adam hesitated.

"Ah. I have placed the finger at the heart of the matter. Who is she? Spit it out."

A flush of red crept over Adam's neck. He shook his head. "It's not as you think. Besides, it's too early to speak of those matters. One should not spill the beans before the day is over. Besides, you will only mock and tease me for the rest of the day."

There was a serious look on St Addington's face. "I do hope that you know me better than that. You know that I would support you with any decision you might make. Even getting married and starting a nursery. If anyone deserves it, it is you."

Adam softened. "No, you are right. I trust you more than anyone, Cousin. But when it comes to courtship.... I am so different from you. I find it quite difficult to talk to women. I tend to get rather shy around ladies. But all you need to do is pull out that charming smile of yours, snap your fingers, and all womankind faints at your feet. I don't think there's another man in London who is being pursued by petticoats as much as you are."

St Addington pulled a face. "The way you put it, somehow that doesn't sound like a compliment."

"I'm sorry, Cousin. But it's true, isn't it? You have no problems courting ladies. Contrary to you, I don't care about looks. I am looking for an honest connection of the heart. Something sincere. Long lasting. Something that might actually bring me happiness. Maybe even love. That is somewhat more difficult to find."

"I agree."

Adam looked at him, surprised. "Do you?"

"Well, yes. All I have to do is snap my fingers," he snapped his fingers, "And, as you say, the women fall adoringly to my feet. Widows, bits of muslin, doxies, and all kinds of ladies. One hanging from each of my fingers. One hardly knows what to do with them all. It does tend to grow rather tedious." He put on a pensive look. "Should I go for that lady in pink, you think? Or that one in moss green? Too difficult a choice? Well then, let me snap my fingers again and see who else falls to my feet. Maybe my luck's better this time. Or not."

Adam threw him a searching look. "I would wish that for once, just once, you put that mask of yours away and speak seriously. I know deep down you're not really like that. Sometimes you play the fool even in private, and to be honest, Adrian, I don't like it." He walked to the door.

"Adam."

Adam paused, his hand on the handle of the door.

"I'm sorry." St Addington hesitated. "I said I wouldn't mock you, and then I went ahead and did precisely that."

"I know you too well, Cousin."

"I can assist you, if you want."

"You mean to snap the fingers for me?" A small smile flitted over Adam's face. "I am not sure that would work out so well. If you will excuse me, I have a letter to write."

"Another one? You write too much these days. Do you care to share it with me if I promise not to mock you?"

"Don't take it personally, Cousin. But no. Not yet."

St Addington got up and stretched himself. "I will patiently wait until you reveal the lady's identity to me, then. In the meantime, I'll be off to the club. Gamble a bit. Get drunk. Maybe climb into some lonely lady's boudoir and get called out by her husband the next morning." He yawned. "Business as usual."

Adam clucked his tongue. "You know that is not true."

"What is not?"

"What you just said. All this snapping of your fingers part. I was just funning. Just because they expect you to

34

be the eternal rake doesn't mean you have to play the part." And with those words, he left.

The knuckles of St Addington's fingers on his cup whitened.

"Oh, but I do," he whispered.

Chapter Five

"LUDMILLA." AUNT ERNESTINA LOOKED HER OVER with her quizzing glass. "Let me look at you."

They were in Aunt Ernestina's Residence in Rutherford House at Grosvenor Square, London. Ernestina had great plans for Lu, which included a complete overhaul of her appearance.

Lu quaked in her shoes and awaited the verdict.

"I daresay you have increased the number of freckles on your nose. No doubt you have been sitting in the glaring sunlight. Mary," Ernestina snapped her fingers, and the abigail appeared magically. "Make sure to anoint her face three times a day with Gowland's Lotion. It is supposed to work miracles when it comes to getting rid of freckles." Turning back to Lu, she clucked and said, "I really cannot comprehend it. Why would you insist on always dressing in those horrid colours?"

"Mother insisted that they suit my complexion." The browns and khaki colours had been for her, whereas her sister Jessica was dressed in pastels and pinks.

"Bah. The woman must have been colour blind. No wonder you are still a spinster, running around like you do. For heaven's sake, child, take off that cap. How old are you again?"

"Twenty-eight, Aunt Ernestina. I daresay old enough to warrant a cap."

"Poppycock. Mary."

"Yes, my lady."

"Take the thing and burn it."

"But Aunt!" Lu exclaimed, scandalised.

Mary looked at Lu expectantly to take off the cap. She clung to it as if her life depended on it. Mary pulled, and after a few tugs, Lu let go.

Lu looked after the maid despondently as she disappeared with a significant symbol of Lu's old, staid, but peaceful life.

"You are no Windmere beauty," Aunt Ernestina concluded.

Lu's chin went up defiantly. She'd heard this her entire life. That she never measured up to the others. Before she could blurt out that she was *glad* she was no Windmere beauty, and that she did not want to look like a china doll with golden baby-curls, Aunt Ernestina sniffed. "However, as much as it pains me, it must be said. With proper grooming, proper clothes and proper posture—must you forevermore stoop like an old woman? —and proper food—you *must* plump up more—you would look a decently fetching thing."

Lu gasped. Did Aunt Ernestina just call her decently fetching? That was almost equivalent to pretty.

"But Aunt—"

Aunt Ernestina lifted her hand. "I fail to understand why you would think otherwise. No Windmere woman has ever been unsightly, unless she makes herself so. Yes, we Windemere women are exceptional beauties. Including myself."

It was true. Ernestina was a handsome woman, tall, imposing, good complexion and not a single grey hair on her auburn head. But that may be because she dyed it with henna.

"Not all men are amenable to tall blondes with baby ringlets. Keep that in mind. Your figure and colouring will improve with the right kind of clothes. There is nothing to be done about the black and straight hair, so what can one do but show it off to its best advantage? You, my girl, are a challenge. I like challenges. I will concentrate all my efforts on you, for I daresay Jessica here," Jessica came forward with a dimpled smile, "Yes, our Jessica here will haul in a husband by the end of the month, easily. They will litter the carpet, the earls, and viscounts. It will be most tedious. My advice: go for nothing less than a duke." She patted Jessica's dimpled cheek.

"Yes, Aunt," Jessica said obediently.

Lu rolled her eyes. It had been only the first week in London, and she was thoroughly tired of hearing all about husband-hunting.

"But you. You need some work. I daresay if your mother Helen had trusted you to me to begin with, none of that fiddlefaddle would've happened, and you'd be safely married for a decade already. But after I am done with you, they will come. I owe it to Helen and my poor brother, God rest their souls in peace. It is the last thing I can do for them, to see their children married well. For I *will* have you married off before the end of the season. Mark my words. We are going shopping in an hour. Come, Jessica."

And with those words, she sailed off, taking Lu's sister with her.

"Help," Lu said into the empty room.

LATER THAT AFTERNOON, Aunt Ernestina took them shopping.

Dear me! When Aunt Ernestina went shopping, one needed a fleet of servants to trudge along to carry all the parcels.

Boxes of hats, ribbons, gloves, shawls, unmentionables, stockings, shoes, boots and slippers, morning dresses, afternoon dresses, ballroom gowns, nightgowns, spencers and pelisses, fichus and shawls.

Lu's head whirled. How could a person wear so many clothes? It must have cost a fortune, but Ernestina poohpoohed it away. She reminded her that it was vulgar to mention money in her presence.

Then Ernestina had bullied her into getting a new haircut. Now her straight black hair was short and felt oddly light. It fell across her forehead into her eyes in a most unusual way. She hid it under her bonnet, which Aunt Ernestina eyed with misgiving.

"For heaven's sake, child, drop the horrid brown fabric bolt at once. Why must you forevermore touch things that are brown? And look at the pretty silk here

40

instead." Ernestina lifted a bolt with the most delightful apricot coloured silk to Lu's face.

"This one will do nicely. A shawl as well. With silver trimming."

Now she was in possession of three new morning dresses, two ball gowns, three afternoon dresses and a riding habit. Everything was exhaustingly colourful in blues, pinks and greens. She would stand out like an orchid in a cornfield and not be able to melt into the wallpaper inconspicuously like she planned. People would notice her.

Her stomach churned nervously.

They walked along Berkeley Street, went to Gunter's Tea shop, and strolled across Berkeley Square. Jessica was chattering non-stop when they ran into Lady Randolph, a friend of Aunt Ernestina, who insisted on taking them into the new gloves and hats shop.

Lu sighed. She was quite exhausted from this morning's shopping, and her new boots pinched. She already had a blister on her right heel.

"With your permission, I will remain seated here at this bench with Mary and wait for you." The weak winter sun peeked through the clouds, and it would be pleasant to sit outside for a while. She hadn't had too much sunshine when living with Mildred, and now she took advantage of turning her face toward the sun any time she had the opportunity. The shop was not far away. Mary, who'd been carrying all the bandeau boxes and bags, looked grateful.

"Very well. Mind you, make sure to use the parasol to keep new freckles from forming on your nose. We will need a while. I see they have a new collection of bonnets. We will pick up several for you as well."

"Without ostrich feathers, please, Aunt, and nothing in purple or turquoise—" Lu said hastily, but they had already disappeared into the shop.

The bench was next to a marble statue. Lu approached it, curious, and read the name on the plaque. "The Duke of Quimble." A jolt went through her.

The statue of the Duke of Quimble! How Addy had mocked it in his letters!

The Duke of Quimble has the most unfortunate visage. A potato for a nose and cauliflowers for ears. I am convinced the artist intended to revenge himself on his patron by making him as hideous looking as possible, a caricature, almost. You must see it, Lu. It is in the middle of the square and not too far from my home. I am most unfortunate to have to pass it every day on the way to my club.

Lu's heart started to hammer.

She knew Addy's address by heart.

Bruton Street 4B.

If Addy's directions were correct, the street must be nearby.

Mary was dozing on the bench. Lu's feet started to move of their own volition.

From the square to the right—there was Bruton Street.

A quiet, fashionable street with oak trees. A row of dapper, identical-looking town houses with black iron fencing framed the street.

And one of these was Addy's.

She counted the houses. It was easily found.

Lu stood in front of 4B with a dry mouth. She stood by the lamp pole with a thudding heart. What would happen if she were to walk up the stairs to the big black lacquered door, knock with the golden knocker, and ask for Addy?

Lu played it out in her mind. The butler would open the door, look at her inquiringly, and—

The door opened.

Lu jumped. Goodness gracious! Now she'd willed the door to open through sheer wishful thinking! She pressed herself against the lamp pole, hoping she was invisible.

Out came a tall, exquisitely dressed gentleman in a top hat and Hessian boots. A nonpareil. A gentleman of the first ranks. A pink of the ton. Complete with attitude as well. Aloof. Arrogant. Awe-inspiring. The kind of man who thoroughly intimidated her.

His glance brushed over her—and dismissed her. It was a glance she was altogether familiar with. She knew what they saw. A spinster with a nondescript brown bonnet and pelisse. A nobody, colourless, forgetful. She cringed.

No! She would not cringe. Lu forced herself upright, to meet his eyes, but he'd already passed and forgotten her. He strolled down the street, twirling his cane in his gloved hands. A coal boy jumped out of his way, and another fellow pulled his hat, making a fawning obeisance, but the dandy ignored him.

Her mind was in jumbles. This wasn't Addy, for sure, it couldn't be. He'd been too arrogant to be Addy. It could be anyone. A visitor. Of course! It must be a visitor.

A woman from the neighbouring house, a servant, came out.

"Pray, tell me, whose house is this?" Lu's voice was breathless.

The woman threw her a curious look. "This is Lord St Addington's abode. Everyone knows that." The woman proceeded to walk down the street with a basket under her arms.

Lu gasped and pressed her hand against her heart.

Even Lu had heard of St Addington. The Wicked Viscount. London's worst rakehell. Lu looked after the retreating figure in confusion. There must be some mistake. Maybe she got the number wrong.

Lu counted again. But no. It definitely was 4B. She was certain, absolutely certain that this was Addy's address. She'd written it too many times.

Why on earth was Addy living with the Wicked Viscount?

Maybe he was a guest there.

That must be it, yes.

But a guest for three years? How odd was that?

That face. That figure! There was something about him that niggled at her memory. As she traced her steps back to the square, her mind set to work furiously.

Where had she seen that face before?

She was certain she'd seen him before.

Once. A long time ago.

That dishevelled golden hair, curling at the nape, those icy blue-green eyes.

Slouching in an armchair, loosened cravat, one booted leg draped over the armrest. A man ought not be so cruelly beautiful.

His thin lips pulled into a sarcastic, provocative smile.

He'd been drunk.

Hadn't he been in Matthew Frederick's circle of friends? Charming Matthew, with his cheerful smile and light-hearted demeanour. Her heart weighed down with the memory of what might have been. She brushed it away.

Back to the matter at hand. Yes, that's where she'd seen him. He must have been one of Matthews's friends.

She froze to a statue in the middle of the street as the memory rushed back to her and everything came together.

"Ten guineas only? Paltry. A hundred. What do you say, St Addington?" Matthew taunted.

"I wager the double. Nay, the triple." The man with the icy eyes and the angelic locks had replied.

St Addington.

Addington.

Addy.

Lu's world tilted.

Chapter Six

In a trance, Lu made her way back to the bench, where Mary was still dozing.

She dropped on the bench next to her and felt like she was about to throw up.

Her best friend, with whom she'd corresponded the past three years, was London's worst rakehell, who wasted his fortune on wine, women, and song.

St Addington. She hated him with a passion.

Thanks to him, she was a spinster.

No, no, no, no, no! It couldn't be possible. St Addington wasn't Addy. He just wasn't.

She didn't believe it. She refused to believe it! It was altogether impossible. She knew Addy, her Addy. St Addington had none of these qualities that she so loved in Addy. Her Addy was charming, intelligent, witty, and *kind*. He'd even confessed that deep down, he was shy. He had a fantastic sense of humour. He was bookish. They shared the same taste in books! He couldn't possibly be a wicked rake. Rakes didn't read books. That tulip she'd seen had never picked up a book in his entire life.

Addy wasn't that awful St Addington, the man who'd challenged Matthew with a drunken drawl. *"I bet you a hundred guineas even you can't work up the courage to kiss the homeliest Windmere woman with your eyes open."* The raunchy laughter that followed.

Oh! The humiliation! Lu pressed her hands against her burning cheeks as she relived the memory.

The homeliest Windmere woman.

That was what he'd called her.

The words had burned into her mind and left a bitter acid taste in her mouth.

Horrible, horrible, horrible man!

But...what if the impossible was true and St Addington indeed was Addy....

Merciful heavens!

Her hand crawled to her heart.

The things *he* knew about *her*!

Almost everything. She'd bared her soul to him like no other.

Lu groaned so loud that a man who walked past her jumped aside in surprise.

She wished she could turn into that hazel bush and never speak—or rather write—to another living being again.

Her only consolation was that he did not know her real name. She'd been careful never to reveal it. Nor did he know what she looked like.

For if he knew...if he knew...that she was that homeliest Windmere woman...the one he'd so mocked, whom he couldn't bear to kiss with eyes open...

Lu took a big breath and exhaled shakily. It was unthinkable.

Refocus, Lu. Refocus.

Let us analyse the facts. What did she really know about Addy?

He was pathetically afraid of spiders. His dog was a bloodhound called Macbeth. He had a sharp, wicked sense of humour. He liked it when rain pitter-pattered against the windowpanes. He fell off a donkey when he was a child and had a scar on his right elbow. Since then, he was mortally afraid of donkeys (in addition to spiders). Their very brawl made him break out in a sweat of fear. An involuntary chuckle escaped Lu. He was shy and preferred to read books over attending balls. His favourite book was *Robinson Crusoe*. He wanted to *be* Robinson Crusoe. Except he could not imagine leaving the comforts of his parlour and forgoing his tea. He liked to drink tea that was excessively sweet. He liked sugar plums. He could recite the entire collection of Pope's poetry by heart. He probably sat in front of the fireplace the entire evening, reading books, reciting Pope, drinking his sweet tea, listening to the rain prattle onto the windowpane, like an old man.

Or did he?

How could she know that for sure? What if Addy read books in front of the fireplace—for, say, five minutes —then got up to spend the remaining night seducing women at a gaming hell?

Lord St Addington. What did she know about him? He was said to spend his entire time in dens of sin and vice. He ruined perfectly respectable women and debutantes merely by looking at them. Men lost their entire fortunes to him. He won entire estates, while the poor men who lost to him shot themselves at dawn. He'd fleeced the Prince Regent himself. Even Napoleon had no chance against him. It was said the emperor of the French had lost a game of piquet against him in the middle of the battlefield, while the cannonballs zoomed by their ears. He duelled with outraged cuckolded husbands on a weekly basis, and one had lost count of how many he'd shot dead. The number of widows in London had dramatically increased on account of him. Once, he himself died, only to mysteriously reappear without a scratch in a gaming hell the next morning. Then, he was said to break into a damsel's bedroom at midnight in Mayfair, while at the same time abducting another from her boudoir in Bloomsbury. Only St Addington managed to be in two places at the same time— he was said to be the devil incarnate, the fallen angel, Lucifer manifested. He certainly looked the part.

Lu chewed on her fingernails. A lot of that was obviously tosh and nonsense. Gossip, rumours, a bag of moonshine. It was likely that none of it was true.

Or was it?

Fact was: Addy, her Addy, had nothing to do with all that.

But...how could she know for sure?

What if the only thing she knew for sure was that he wrote lovely letters? What if she'd painted an image of him that didn't exist? What if Addy never existed outside of her own mind?

What if he'd lied to her all along?

But how could a man like St Addington write such charming, witty letters?

Yet the ultimate nut she found hard to swallow was: how could a man like St Addington be her best friend?

"What balderdash. This can't be true." She noticed too late that she'd spoken out loud.

"Lu! Did you just swear?" Aunt Ernestina had grown out of the ground like a toadstool and frowned. They'd finished shopping. "Only eccentrics are allowed to swear publicly, remember that. You, my girl, have not yet acquired that status." Aunt Ernestina sniffed. "And if I have anything to say in the matter, you shan't, ever. Though you are getting mightily close to it."

"Yes, Aunt."

"Take off that mangled bonnet of yours. We obtained you a more fetching one." She held out a yellow bonnet of straw, silk, and feathers. It was cheerful and frilly and altogether not what Lu tended to wear.

She obediently tied the sun-yellow ribbons around her face.

"There. Unbelievable what a difference a bonnet makes. You look ten years younger, child. Let us return home. Then tea, then rest, then we must prepare for the Whittlesborough ball. It will be such a crush, and you need to be seen."

"Seen? But why?" Under no circumstances did she want to be seen!

"Naturally, you need to be seen so you can get married."

The horror!

"But I really don't want to get married, Aunt," Lu wailed. Some pedestrians turned their heads towards them in curiosity. She considered running all the way back to Bath, on foot, if she needed to. She'd lock herself up in the safety of the dark, dank tomb that was her Great Aunt Mildred's house, where she never needed to be seen by anyone, nor to get reminded that Addy might be that terrible viscount.

"Fiddlesticks. Of course you want to get married. It is high time that you do. Now, Ludmilla. Get into the carriage. I shall tell Mary you will wear the pink dress at the ball."

Lu felt something rebelling inside her at her aunt's infantilizing of her. "Pink, Aunt. Really?"

"Yes, really. It will suit your complexion admirably."

"But the ball is in two days?" Lu countered. "Why do we have to prepare already?"

"One cannot start too early with preparations," countered her aunt.

"I am so excited; do you think the Prince Regent is attending as well?" Jessica asked.

"The entire world will be there, my girl." Her aunt sniffed.

"Even Lord St Addington?" Lu hadn't meant to ask. She really hadn't. It'd just popped out of her mouth.

Ernestina raised an eyebrow. "Especially him. It's his hunting ground."

"No," breathed Jessica. "How exciting!"

"Exciting, poppycock. He is a terrible rake but of good stock, mind you. He is worth a fortune. He is London's most eligible bachelor and many a match-making mama have desperately tried and failed to get him to come up to scratch. Alas, he is a hopeless case. Nonetheless, we have to try."

"We? Try?" Lu's mouth fell open.

"Close your mouth, Lu. It is always good to be seen in the company of a viscount, even if he is a terrible rake-hell. He will come in very useful at the Whittlesborough ball. I will make sure he will dance at least once with Jessica. Naturally, I shall have to invite him for a supper party. He won't refuse since Hector and he were schoolmates."

"Good Heavens, Aunt. Are you certain Jessica's reputation won't be tarnished when she is seen in his company?" Under no circumstances did she want her to dance with St Addington.

"Poppycock. He has no taste for insipid debutantes, so Jessica will be safe. And you will try your best to remain unimpressed by his flirtations. For flirt he will, make no mistake about that. There is a reason why he has acquired that reputation of his. Be on your guard."

"Yes, Aunt," Lu swallowed.

Chapter Seven

By the time they reached the home in Grosvenor Square, Lu had come to a monumental conclusion.

The only way for her to know for sure whether Addy was really Lord St Addington was to write to him—and to accept his suggestion of meeting him somewhere. Without him knowing who she was. She had no idea how to meet him and simultaneously keep her identity a secret. But this way, she would be mentally and emotionally better prepared when they actually met at the ball, or, heaven forbid, at her aunt's supper party.

She would simply have to write the note without her address on it.

Lu pulled on her lower lip. The question was, where would be a good place to meet?

"You seem awfully absent-minded lately, Lu. Is anything the matter?" Jessica had come into her room and chattered on and on about this and that. There was an air of suppressed excitement about her. She could not sit still for five minutes, but jumped up, took a turn about the room, touched a vase, picked up a hand mirror, and set the pillows askew. She had two hectic spots on her cheeks and looked even more beautiful than usual. Lu supposed she was excited because of the Whittlesborough ball tomorrow.

"No, nothing's the matter. I've just been thinking."

"What about? Tell me." Jessica stood in front of her with a shawl in her hand and looked at her expectantly.

"Where would you go and meet someone you hardly knew? In London, I mean," Lu suddenly burst out. She hadn't meant to say it, but there she was. "If you did not want them to call on you, but, maybe, just take a short stroll together. Nothing that expresses too much of an immediate commitment."

Jessica did not think this question was strange at all. "Easy. There are so many places. One of the parks. Or in a museum." She thought. "I know the very place. There is a lovely green bench in front of the new circulating library, right in front of Hyde Park. You can take a walk into the park from there."

Lu thought quickly. It seemed like a good plan.

"In fact, I've been meeting some people there myself," Jessica's voice trailed off. "I did not want them calling on me. Don't tell Aunt Ernestina, though, will you?"

"Of course not." Lu threw her a sharp look. "Is there something you'd like to tell me? You seem so, I don't know. Overly excited. Is it because of the ball tomorrow?"

"Oh, Lu." Jessica sat down on the bed and placed

both hands over her cheeks. "I am so confused! I think I may be in love."

"Dear me!" Lu's eyes widened. "Who is it?"

"A gentleman of the first order. I have never met anyone like him! Oh, he is not only terribly good-looking, but also very manly." There were stars in Jessica's eyes. "I was crossing Bond Street, and there were so very many carriages. I don't know what happened, but I must've stumbled over a stone, and I fell. And oh! A curricle was racing right towards me, and so fast, too!"

Lu blanched.

"The horses were galloping directly towards me, and would you believe it, Lu, I was veritably frozen, I couldn't do anything at all but lie there and stare stupidly into the face of certain death." Jessica shuddered dramatically.

"And then?" Lu shook her arm. "Continue!"

The dreamy, starry look entered Jessica's eyes again. "And then *he* came, like a guardian angel, and picked me up like I weighed nothing at all and carried me to the other side of the street. Just in time, for the curricle thundered by not a second later. If he hadn't saved me, I'd certainly be dead now even as we speak."

"Good heavens, Jessica! You were not hurt, were you?"

"Not even a scratch. I'd not even twisted my ankle, though part of me wished I did, so that he could carry me all the way home."

"Jessica!" Lu sounded scandalised. "Well, whoever he was, we owe him your life for sure!"

"Yes, this is what I keep saying. He is my guardian angel."

"Do you know who it was?"

"This is the thing, Lu. I don't know." Her violet eyes clouded over and shifted aside. Then they lifted and met Lu's straight on. "But I can't help but think of him every waking minute of the day. Oh, Lu! At night I even dream of him."

Lu shifted uncomfortably. "Goodness. It does seem to be a strong case of infatuation."

"And I look out for him everywhere we go. On the street, the places we visit..." Jessica's voice trailed off. "I am certain I will meet him tomorrow at the Whittlesborough ball."

Lu patted her hand. "If he is there, you must introduce us."

"Lu. Please don't tell anything to Aunt. She would disapprove, and that would break my heart."

DEAR ADDY,

At last, we are in London. And all my fears have come to pass. My aunt has become unhinged and is dragging me to every single shop in town. Every. Single. Shop. She insists I dress like a peacock in the most impossible colours, like pink and purple and green because "they suit my complexion". Yes, let us meet and take a turn about Hyde Park. Tomorrow at three. Do you know the bench in front of the circulating library? I shall await you there.

Never mind what she'd just suggested was highly improper.

No lady who cared for her reputation would ever ask a gentleman to meet her alone.

Lu decided it did not matter.

For of course, she wouldn't be there to meet him.

She would be safely hiding inside the library across the street and watch from the window which gentleman was waiting.

Lu thought it was an excellent plan.

Her heart hammered. Addy, of course, wouldn't be able to reply because he did not know who to direct it to. There would be no return address on the missive, and she'd heavily bribed her footman to post the missive anonymously from a post office in London, rather than deliver it in person.

Then, she pulled out the letters she'd received from Addy. Yes, she'd taken them all along with her to London, safely stowed away in a mahogany box inlaid with mother of pearl.

With shaking hands, she unfolded several letters and inspected the signature.

She shook her head. To her, the scribble read "Addy".

But certainly, it was a scrawl of a signature that left the "Y" in a long, flourishing loop... she'd always considered it to be ornamental. For the first time, it dawned on her that it could've been an omission, a lazy way of signing the remaining half of his name: —ington.

He'd always signed with his complete name: Addington.

She'd completely misunderstood and misread Addy.

With shaking hands, Lu refolded her letters and stowed them away in the box and buried it in the depths of her wardrobe.

Chapter Eight

Lu told her aunt the truth, namely that she wanted to go to a circulating library to obtain some books.

"Are you going to the Temple of the Muses?" Jessica looked up from her embroidery.

"It is that new circulating library across from Hyde Park you told me about," Lu explained. "Although I was thinking we could also stop by the Temple of the Muses on the way."

"How vexatious! I have a previous commitment with Miss Edith Townsend. She's invited me to go shopping with her."

"More shopping!" Lu shuddered.

"Apparently her ribbons don't match the ball dress, and I offered to accompany her."

"Never mind. I shall take Mary with me," Lu added hastily, before her aunt could object. She'd expected a tirade on bluestockings and how it wasn't good that one read so much, but her aunt surprised her.

"Very well, Ludmilla. You may pick up a novel for me. One by that Radcliffe woman. *The Mysteries of Udolpho* would do nicely."

This left Lu speechless.

They arrived at the library a quarter of an hour before the appointed time. Lu sent Mary away on an errand and asked her to return within the hour. She pushed the door open and inhaled the typical smell of books, paper, dust, and ink. There were only a few people inside. Lu hovered close to the shelves next to the display window, looking nervously through the glass at the street, from where she could see the bench next to the oak tree.

She hadn't counted on there being so many people near the bench. It seemed to be a popular meeting place. There were several people standing around, chatting with each other, sitting on the bench next to the lamp pole.

Lu took book after book off the shelf without really seeing what they were, until she held an entire pile on her arms. Her eyes were glued to the bench outside.

There! A gentleman in grey walked up. He was slight, of middle height, light blond hair under a top hat. Her age. Possibly older.

Lu's heart hammered.

He sat down on the bench, crossed his legs, then pulled out a pocket watch and looked at it.

Lu stretched her neck to see him clearly.

This, she realised with a sudden shock, must be Addy.

It wasn't St Addington. The feeling of relief that

rushed through her left her so giddy that she leaned against the bookshelf and closed her eyes, sending up a quiet prayer of thanks.

He got up and walked up and down, clearly waiting for someone. How fine he looked. A sigh escaped Lu. Just like she'd imagined. Handsome, kind, a high intellectual forehead. At least from this vantage point. He kept looking at his pocket watch, then up the street, turned, looked down the street. Walked back and forth again. Lu's mind started to work. How to proceed from here? She felt a sudden urge to rush outside and greet him, like an old friend. They were friends, weren't they? Then she remembered how inconspicuous, almost drab she looked. She'd put on her old bonnet and her old pelisse, knowing she would be invisible if dressed thus. She regretted it now. Oh, why oh why hadn't she put on one of her new dresses that her aunt had insisted on buying for her? What if Addy was disappointed when he saw her? She felt a pang. She would die if she saw a look of embarrassment in his eyes, followed by some polite excuse to leave. It would be awkward. Lu bit on her lips. She saw his profile. Oh dear. There was an expression of impatience crossing his face. She'd let him wait for already a quarter of an hour. She got on her toes to get a better view, it looked like he turned, and if he could turn only a bit more, she would see his face—

"Excuse me. You seem to have dropped these."

"What?"

She looked up, right into a pair of sardonically blue-green eyes.

Lu felt all the colour drain from her face. Her heart

nearly jumped out of her chest. She may have emitted a squeak.

"You have dropped these books." He bent to pick them up. "*The Imaginary Adulteress.*" A corner of his lips quirked. "Charming."

Lucy choked and snatched the book out of his hands. "I was looking for a book for my aunt." Surprisingly, she managed to put a coherent sentence together.

"No doubt *The Imaginary Adulteress* is an excellent choice. Or is it to be—" he flipped the second book to read the title. "*The Nunnery for Coquettes?*" He tsked and lifted an eyebrow in mock amusement. "I must say, I cannot account for the reading taste of your aunt, but I find myself inexplicably drawn to *The Imaginary Adulteress.* In fact, now I positively feel I must read it. May I?" He held out a hand.

With burning cheeks, she handed him the book.

He pulled off his gloves, finger by finger, and flipped through the book.

This wasn't happening. Lu wasn't really standing inside this library discussing *risqué* books with none other than the Viscount St Addington.

Her breath came in shallow gasps, and she felt dizzy.

Oh no! Now her mind was going round and round again in a heated jumble. She felt hot, and Mary had definitely strung her corset too tightly this morning, for she could barely breathe.

The man was standing far too close as he perused the book. His cologne smelled musky and nice, and it caused an odd kind of tingling in her stomach that she did not want to think about just now.

She fanned herself with a book and glanced out of the window.

Addy was gone. He'd left, likely cross that she had not shown up. A pang shot through her. Her first instinct was to run outside to see where he'd gone. But instead, she remained glued to the spot, staring at *him*. His hat sat at a rakish angle on a head of dishevelled curls, and he wore a well-tailored grey tailcoat with breeches that clung to his thighs, and a pair of well-polished Hessians.

Lu was certain he was the same man who'd lounged in that armchair and challenged Matthew. So long ago.

She wondered whether he even remembered that. For she certainly did.

Her mind was in a confused jumble. Humiliation. Anger. Fear. And something else that she could not pinpoint.

Dear me, he'd just asked her something, and she hadn't paid attention, judging from the inquisitive, amused look on his face.

"I just asked whether you are certain you want to borrow this book, otherwise I would claim it," he said, holding the volume in his long, white fingers.

"Are you certain you are a reader?" That snippy comment came across her lips before she could stop herself.

Both his eyebrows shot up. "My dear," he drawled, "come and think of it, I may not be so certain I can read at all. I do imagine I may have learned my alphabet once upon a time. I can't recall for sure because it was so long ago. In fact, I may decide to get this book only to look at the pictures. One can't help but enjoy looking at—

pictures. They are so—pretty." He stared deeply into her eyes. "The pictures, I mean."

Something hot flushed through her.

"But then," he continued, "contrary to general opinion, I tend to adhere to the notion that books have some sort of purpose other than being read. I can think of all sorts of—uses."

There was no reason at all for this to sound indecent, but somehow it did. It was the way he said it. Lu felt herself flush an even darker shade of red without knowing why. "Oh? Such as?"

"They say dry books make excellent material for a fire." He knocked against the book's spine.

She pulled her lips into a scornful smile.

Insufferable man!

At that moment, she promised herself something. He'd humiliated her once. He'd not do so again. Lu welcomed the feeling of anger that flushed through her. She decided she hated the man.

She snatched the book out of his hands. "I do want it."

"Shame," he replied. "I would have liked it for myself. To look at the pictures."

Oh! That smile! How dare he smile at her like that? As though they shared a delicious secret.

She had to tilt her face upwards to see his eyes. The top of her head reached his shoulder. The man was a mountain.

"What else do you have there?" He leaned against the bookshelf, crossed his arms and blocked her way.

Lu had no idea. She'd just picked books randomly

and clutched them in her arm as if to ward him off. She stared at the books she still held in her hand. "*How It Happened That I Was Born*," she read out loud, stunned. "And '*Twas Wrong To Marry Him.*"

"Dear me." His face was deadpan. "Both sound like they might be stimulating reads."

"What *is* this place?" She looked at the bookshelf, which was crammed with 18th century oddities, *risqué* books that were not considered proper at all.

The ridiculousness of the situation hit her hard. She bit down on her lower lip to keep herself from smiling.

He pulled another book out of the shelf. "*Princess Coquedoef and Prince Bonbon*," he read. A muscle twitched in his jaw. "Well, would you know? I just surprised myself. It appears I possess the ability to read after all."

"Princess—what?"

"Coque-d'oeuf? Or maybe it is Cockydoof," he mused.

An unladylike snort escaped from Lu's lips. She valiantly tried to pull herself together, but it wasn't to be helped.

"The title is most original, I must say. Though nothing compares to this one, here, *The Adventures Of A Pin, Supposed To Be Related By Himself, Herself, Or Itself.*" His voice shook. "I take it back. My ability to read, if I have ever possessed it, has most definitely deserted me, for none of this makes sense whatsoever."

Lu couldn't help herself. She succumbed to a peal of helpless laughter.

He joined in. His laughter was a rich baritone.

"No one," Lu wiped the tears away, "No one writes books like that anymore."

"I wonder which of these you will decide to get for your aunt." His eyes glinted.

"Aunt Ernestina wants me to get her *The Mysteries of Udolpho*, or something else by Ann Radcliffe."

"Oho! Crumbling castles, ghosts, monks, murders, persecuted heroines and the like. I approve. Mind you, not that I have read any of it." He lifted both hands in mock horror. "Not having the capability to read, see."

"Oh, do be quiet," Lu snapped. "You can read very well. I am sorry I implied otherwise, so you needn't rub it in continuously."

He grinned.

She decided to take all of them, including the *Imaginary Adulteress*, not because she was interested in it, but because he insisted till the very last that he wanted it, following her to the counter, trying to wheedle her into giving up the book, which she refused. At this point, she couldn't admit that she did not want this book, even though the title seemed to imply it was highly improper for a lady to read. She would get it and read it merely because he wanted it. For some perverted reason, she felt she had to oppose him in this simple matter.

The clerk's eyebrows shot up when he read the title, and he hastily proceeded to wrap it in newspaper.

No matter.

As the viscount held the door open for her, he flashed the full charm of his smile on her, leaving her speechless.

"Maybe we shall meet again, Miss—" he lifted his hat, waiting for her to fill in her name. She kept quiet.

He shrugged. "Then you must relate to me all about the book. Or what is better, lend it to me."

When she didn't reply, he bowed. "I'm St Addington. Your servant."

She mumbled something unintelligible and fled, dragging Mary along, who had returned from her errand and was waiting by the door.

Two THINGS she'd learned that day.

One: Addy looked exactly like she imagined him to look. He was also cross with her. She'd have to write another note, apologizing and coming up with some sort of excuse why she hadn't shown up at the appointed time.

Two: Lord St Addington was everything they said he was. He was deadly charming. And deadly odious. And deadly attractive.

Her heart skipped a beat.

And she was deadly furious at him. Because of what he'd done to her so long ago.

And she was furious at herself for her heart beating in this irregular manner every time she thought of him, but she could not admit that to herself just now.

IN THE MIDDLE of the night, Lu sat up straight in bed, her heart racing.

She lit the candle with shaking fingers.

The feeling of dread that she'd got everything wrong weighed her down.

What if the gentleman who'd waited outside by the bench wasn't really Addy? What proof did she really have—other than that he matched her vision of Addy—that it was really him? There'd been several people waiting there. How did she know he'd waited for her? He could have waited for someone else. Why had she fixated on that particular gentleman? Because he happened to look nice? Because she wanted him to be Addy so very, very badly?

She could not, ought not ignore the obvious: for it was an extraordinary coincidence, really, that St Addington, the same man she'd seen walking out of the house in Bruton Street, appeared in that lending library when she was supposed to meet Addy. At the same time. The same place.

Why would a man like St Addington visit a dusty old circulating library—unless!

Unless he knew to begin with that Lu was *not* going to meet him at the appointed place.

Unless he knew that Lu would hide in the library and not reveal herself.

Unless he knew that Lu was testing him.

Because no one, no one knew her as well as Addy.

A hot feeling flushed through Lu.

She grudgingly admitted that she and St Addington had shared the same kind of ridiculous humour.

They'd laughed together, between the bookshelves of a circulating library.

She fell back into her pillows with a groan.

Oh no!

That terrible St Addington *must be* Addy after all.
She felt panic crawl over her again.
What on earth was she to do now?

Chapter Nine

"Where the blazes have you been all afternoon?" St Addington asked his cousin as he strolled into the drawing room and found Adam slouching in an armchair with a glass of burgundy.

Adam looked up briefly. "I also had an arrangement to meet someone. But my appointment did not show." He lifted a finger to call the butler. "Has a letter arrived for me?"

"No, sir," the butler replied.

"Strange." Adam rubbed his temple.

"I thought we'd agreed to go to the club later in the afternoon."

"I know. I'd honestly forgotten. I'm sorry." He slumped further into the armchair. "I'm not feeling quite the thing. Maybe I am coming down with the flu."

"I take it your appointment was a lady?" St Addington strolled over to the cart with liquors and poured himself a glass of brandy.

"Yes," Adam said curtly.

"How extraordinarily interesting. The lady you intend to court?" St Addington sat down in a chair and crossed his legs. "The one you intend to set up a nursery with?"

Adam hesitated.

"Now, don't reply with 'No, Maybe, Yes'. I want a straightforward answer, if you please."

"Dash it, I honestly don't know." Adam set down his glass, changed his mind and picked it up and downed its contents in one go. "It's not so easy." He jumped up and strode about the room.

"Things never are when it comes to women. Do you care to tell me about her?" St Addington lifted his hands. "I promise not to say anything overly sarcastic."

Adam hesitated. "We corresponded for a while, and it became clear recently that we may be slowly developing a tendre for each other. We agreed to meet. Yes, I know, improper. This likely being the reason why she did not show. The lady realised it was not the thing, and she's entirely right. End of story. Maybe it's for the best."

"Dashed coincidence, indeed," St Addington echoed. "Life is full of odd coincidences, wouldn't you agree?" St Addington stared absent-mindedly into his brandy. "I wonder who it was you intended to meet?"

"She's not your type at all."

"You should let me decide that for myself."

Adam quirked a quick grin at him that made him look boyish. "So you can snap your fingers and she'll drop at your feet? No thank you."

"You wound me to the quick. My guess is she's the one you've been secretly corresponding with. Yes, I know

74

all about it. You can't keep her identity a secret forever, you know."

Adam flushed. "I know. I promise you, Adrian, when I am more certain about the entire thing, I will let you know. What did you want in that library, by the by?"

"Correct me if I am mistaken, but one commonly tends to obtain books in a library."

"No. Really. Who would have known? St Addington and books?"

"Indeed. The ability with regards to my literacy was recently questioned more than once."

Adam laughed. "You have yourself to blame if you keep on playing the fop. Your acting skills belong on a stage."

"I try, Adam, I try."

"Says the one who got a First in classical literature. You've read this long before I ever did." Adam tapped a finger on a leather tome.

"Yes, but I've long outgrown Cicero et.al." St Addington yawned.

"What about Shakespeare, then? There's a new Hamlet coming to the theatre. Edmund Kean in the role. Do you care to watch it with me? Not tonight, for I feel a headache coming on. But one of these days. You know how much I love the theatre, especially Shakespeare. And Kean is marvellous."

"Certainly, cousin. And tonight? What are you up to now?"

"Reading, what else?" Adam lifted his book.

"Pope. Well, enjoy. I will be off for a game of cards." St Addington picked up his walking stick and attempted to twirl his hat on one end. "On the other hand, I might be off to Covent Garden."

"Madame Beaumont's again?"

"Naturally."

Adam shook his head with a sigh but refrained from commenting.

"Adam."

Their eyes met.

"Quit worrying about me. *'Beauties in vain their pretty eyes may roll; Charms strike the sight, but merit wins the soul.'* By your friend Pope. See? There is hope for me, yet."

Adam sighed again. "I can't help it if you're so bent on stubbornly trudging down that path of self-destruction. I wish—oh, never mind."

St Addington knit his forehead together. "You wish? Tell me. I'm profoundly interested in your thoughts."

"Very well. You'll think me a sentimental fool. I wish you'd forget about the Covent Garden doxies and fall in love with a good woman. There. I said it. No doubt it's because of my own current state of mind. Now, forget that I ever said anything and off you go and enjoy yourself."

"And that I intend to do," St Addington muttered as he jammed his hat on his head. "Love, indeed."

He appeared unusually distracted as he climbed into his carriage.

"To the theatre," he told his coachman.

Chapter Ten

THE WHITTLESBOROUGH BALL WAS A DREADFUL squeeze.

Aunt Ernestina was right when she said the entire world was there, including the Prince Regent. He'd appeared in the middle of the cotillon, causing the musicians to break off mid-music, leaving the dancers to flounder on the ballroom floor. People flocked to the entrance, and all Lu was able to see was the back of a head belonging to a corpulent body clad in uniform. Lu noted that he had a great mane of thick, brown hair, and that was it.

Afterwards, Jessica rushed to her, breathless, with stars in her eyes.

"Lu! Did you see him? Did you see how he stopped and singled me out and kissed my hand?"

She hadn't. "That is wonderful, Jessica. Of course, princes and kings would stop in their tracks to meet my beautiful sister." Lu's smile was sincere. She herself would have hated being singled out in this manner, so she was entirely without jealousy when she uttered those words.

Ernestina was puffed up with pride. "A triumph, Jessica. A triumph. He called you a diamond of the first water. And he is absolutely right, for you are." She fanned herself, highly satisfied.

Jessica looked positively smashing in her pastel blue gown which matched her cornflower blue eyes, and her rich, blonde curls that needed neither crimping nor curling.

Lu supposed she did not look terrible in her apricot-coloured gown, for she'd managed to convince her aunt that apricot was better than pink. Her aunt had eventually relented. It did bring out the colour of her eyes, and her freshly-cut hair bobbed nicely about her face. She'd looked into the mirror earlier and thought the haircut gave her face a nice elfin shape. Her chin was pointed, and she did look younger. Somehow, her aunt's lady's maid had even managed to transform several strands of her straw-straight hair into corkscrew curls that framed her face. That was almost a miracle.

Lu hated being there. The memory of the place was all too recent in her mind. The wallpaper, statues, flower arrangements, the smell of candles and floor waxing, even the footmen were still the same. Lu felt sweat pool in her armpits and wished herself ten leagues away.

She'd been at a ball similar to this one exactly ten years ago. Dressed up as she was now. The only difference was that she hadn't been a wallflower yet, and she'd thought herself in love.

She'd been eighteen, a greenhorn, wide-eyed, curious,

eager to dance. She thought she hadn't looked so bad in her pale green gown, either.

No one had stood up with her.

Dance after dance passed, and she'd shifted impatiently from one foot to another. Her dancing card was empty, but she was not really worried, for she knew her parents would introduce her to eligible gentlemen to dance with.

Except her mother was standing by the side, busily chatting with a group of ladies, having forgotten she was there; her father was in the card room, and little Jessica, only eight, was at home, asleep.

She'd tapped her slipper on the floor along the beat of the music and watched the couples form on the dance floor. How she wished she could join them!

Then he stood in front of her.

Matthew. In his scarlet uniform, with thick, wavy chestnut hair and melting brown eyes, a slight smile about his lips, with Lady Bentley on his arm. She was an acquaintance of Lu's father.

"Ludmilla. This gentleman here begs for an introduction. Lady Ludmilla Windmere, this is Captain Matthew Fredericks. His father is the Earl of Hamchester."

Lu curtsied.

He bowed. "May I ask for this dance?"

Lu's heart quickened as she took his arm, and he led her to the dance floor.

Goodness, how they danced.

If there was something Lu was good at, it was dancing, even though she rarely did so. She was light-footed and had a good rhythm. And she loved the music. It became a part of her when she danced.

With Captain Matthew Fredericks, it hadn't been just any dance. It had been the waltz. She'd felt she was floating on clouds. And he'd asked her for not one, but two dances.

He was a light-hearted, cheerful person. He was, the ton considered, a good catch.

He'd flirted with her, smiled into her eyes, and allowed his hand to brush over hers in a caressing way.

Lu had fallen head over heels in love with him.

The next evening, at another ball, was a repeat of the same. He flirted, they danced, Lu was on clouds. Her mother, the duchess, was jubilant. Lu had made a fantastic catch; she did not even have to do as much as lift her finger.

"What did I tell you, Lu, you will be married before the season is out." Her mother was satisfied.

The day after the ball, Matthew hadn't called, but he'd sent flowers. Red roses. The message couldn't have been clearer.

The third ball, a week later ... had been the Whittlesborough ball.

Lu had looked forward to it with growing anticipation. She'd worn a silver gown and silver ballroom slippers. She felt beautiful. She'd pinched her cheeks until they looked red, and her eyes sparkled. She looked for Matthew. He'd wanted her to reserve the first waltz for him. The orchestra began to play, and he wasn't here. But she'd seen him only a moment ago, a flash of scarlet by the door.

Lu went out into the hallway and heard a burst of laughter come out of the card room.

Maybe he was there?

He was, indeed. Surrounded by his cronies. Lu looked at them uneasily. The company he kept did not look very proper at all. Some gentlemen appeared drunk and could barely stand straight.

Especially that blond-haired one with the icy blue-green eyes, who lounged in an armchair with a leg draped over the armrest.

"You're not in love with her, are you?" he said provocatively, swirling his glass, so that some of the liquid slopped onto the carpet.

"By George. No! With those looks?" Matthew laughed sharply.

"But you are courting her."

Matthew shrugged. "I have to court someone. You know I'm skint. Skinter than a mudlark who digs in the Thames. By Jove. Might as well be her. She's a duke's daughter, got the plumpest dowry of 'em all, even though she's as flat chested as a washboard and not much to look at."

"Let me see if I got this right," St Addington slurred. "You think she's the homeliest Windmere of the lot, but you'll marry her anyhow. For the blunt. And after the wedding night, you'll dispose of her in the country some-where and turn back to pretty, plump Ellen the dancer. At least she's got two melons instead of a washboard."

Another burst of raunchy laughter.

Matthew shrugged. "That's the plan."

"Prime." St Addington suddenly sat up, leaned his

elbows on his knees and stared into Matthew's eyes. "Bet you ten guineas when it comes down to it, you can't work up the courage to kiss the homeliest Windmere girl with your eyes open."

The men roared.

"Ten guineas only? Paltry. A hundred. What do you say, St Addington?" Matthew had taunted.

"I wager the double. Nay, the triple."

"And let it be tonight! Within the hour." That came from Lord Anthony, with whom she'd danced after Matthew. She thought he'd been an amiable, even shy sort of man.

Lu had stood right behind them and heard it all.

She gasped when a sharp pain of humiliation pierced through her.

Her blood pounded; her face flushed miserably.

Then St Addington raised his eyes and looked over Matthew's head, laughing. Her eyes locked with St Addington's.

One terrible second stretched into an eternity.

The laughter in his eyes died and was replaced by something that may have been contriteness, but Lu did not have time to analyse their exact expression.

She felt thoroughly violated, her soul shamed, her entire being mocked at, by men she did not even know.

And Matthew laughingly continued to place bets, all the time unaware that she was standing right behind him.

He never knew.

For she whirled around and ran out into the ballroom, past her parents, out into the street, and walked home, sobbing.

She arrived at her home, silver slippers ruined, her hair soaked, rivulets of water running down her face. She shivered.

The next morning, she came down with a fever. She was violently ill, and by the time she recovered her health, the season was over.

She never set foot in a ballroom after that.

And she never saw Matthew again.

IT ALL RUSHED BACK, the pain and humiliation, the betrayal, and the sadness. Lu willed herself to forget it all. But she couldn't help but let her glance rove around the ballroom in search of a tall man in scarlet uniform with chestnut coloured hair ...

With relief, she saw that he was not here.

Neither was St Addington.

She exhaled a shaky sigh.

The orchestra struck up the strains of another cotillion.

Lu pressed herself against the wall, in an attempt to merge with it. If she stood there long enough, immobile, maybe she would turn into one of those marble statues and they would all leave her in peace.

It didn't work.

Her aunt grabbed her arm and pulled her forward, and she had to curtsy to innumerable gentlemen and ladies. Most looked her over, nodded or curtsied back.

"Lady Ludmilla," drawled Lord Norcroft, an elderly gentleman. "I recall. Your father and I used to go hunting together. I miss those times."

Ludmilla did not know whether to smile politely or to look sad, for it was a sad occasion that he could no longer hunt with her father, who was now dead. As a result, she ended up pulling her face into a grimace. "Er, yes," she said.

"Ludmilla! Goodness, we haven't seen you in years. How are you, dear child?" Lady Norcroft drew her aside, and Lu felt something oddly warm in her heart region.

She conversed with the Norcrofts and thought that maybe this was not so awful after all. There was someone who remembered her kindly.

Even better, no one had asked her to dance. And Lu was fine with that. Even though the music was lovely, and her toes had a tendency to tap on the floor. But she was used to being a wallflower.

No one dared snub her when she was in Aunt Ernestina's company. And Jessica attracted attention a-plenty for both.

They all drifted over to Jessica and the gentlemen surrounding her. Lu looked at her younger sister with pride. Aunt Ernestina was right. She would be engaged before the season was out.

Lu stood right next to the footman who held a tray of ratafia. She took a glass. As she sipped from it, if she could take a tiny step aside, toward the door, then another one, and another one, she would gradually reach the door and—

"Where are you slinking off to, Ludmilla?" There was no way she could escape her aunt's hawkish eyes.

"To powder my nose, Aunt."

"Very well. Be sure to return imminently, as the next

dance will start soon." Her eyes drifted over the crowd. "I see young Marling over there. I will tell him to dance with you." She would bully him into dancing with her. Poor Marling.

Lu swallowed. "Yes, Aunt."

Lu fled to the retiring room, still clutching the glass. She would have to spend the next half an hour there to wait out the next dance.

Shortly before opening the door, she paused. She heard the gaggle of women's voices inside. They'd be preening themselves, gossiping, eyeing each other, judging each other.

Lu's feet automatically walked past the door, down the corridor. Her slippers slid along the floor, first slowly, then faster as the music receded. She turned the corner.

The music and gaggle of voices fell away.

Lu took a deep breath. Ah, blessed, blessed silence.

She was in a gallery. Portraits hung on one side of the wall, rows and rows of eagle-nosed Whittlesboroughs frowning down upon her.

Lu frowned back. She heard footsteps approaching from the other side of the gallery.

Without thinking, she opened the first door on the left, slid inside quietly and closed the door.

Lu looked around, inordinately pleased with herself. She stood in the library.

This is where she would hide until the ball was over. Shortly before midnight, she would reappear, ready to go home with her aunt. What a perfect plan.

Lu studied the rows and rows of bookshelves. She inhaled the smell of dust and paper and shivered with pleasure. A longcase pendulum clock stood between two windows. This. This was her home. She let her fingers trail over the book spines. One has to say one thing for the Whittlesboroughs, their library had substance.

She pulled out a leather-bound book, sniffed it, opened it—and froze.

Someone else was in the library.

Lu held her breath.

There it was again.

Most definitely, a gentle snore.

She turned and silently tiptoed further into the room.

There was a sofa in the middle of the room, with two ottomans by the side and a coffee table. The sofa's back faced her.

A pair of long legs in buckled dancing shoes dangled over the arm of the sofa.

A man, dressed to perfection, was sleeping there.

St Addington.

Chapter Eleven

Lu stared down at the handsome face of St Addington. Why on earth was he here, sleeping? Why hadn't she noticed him earlier?

Fascinated, she bent over him.

He had indecently long eyelashes. They curled in a way that would make a girl envious. They were almost white-blond. As were his eyebrows. What business did a man have to have such pretty eyebrows? And the curve of those lips. Like painted by an artist.

Surely, surely this wasn't Addy? The Addy with whom she'd corresponded for over three years.

"I bet you a hundred guineas even you can't work up the courage to kiss the homeliest Windmere woman."

Her Addy would never have said something as cruel as this.

Never.

Suddenly, all the old emotions, the hurt, the humiliation flushed through her, in addition to something she hadn't felt in a long time: fury.

Regardless of whether he was—or was not—Addy: how dare he? How dare he lie here like that, like sleeping beauty, unaware of her and the hurt he'd caused her in the past?

She still clutched her glass of ratafia, which she'd all but forgotten.

The glass was three-quarters full.

There was no one else in the room.

She could have her revenge.

It was petty and very, very childish.

A small smile flitted over her face.

She tilted her hand.

The ratafia trickled on his face, over his nose, his eyes.

He spluttered, jerked up with a shout, flailed around with his arms. He rubbed his face with his sleeve, cursing. Then he saw Lu standing in front of him. "You?"

"Lawks," she said softly.

"Blast it, woman. What the blazes has come over you to pour this stuff over me?" He scowled as he flicked the liquid from his eyes.

"I must have stumbled. My slippers. A snag in the carpet—" she made a helpless motion with one hand, the other still held the glass with ratafia, and he jerked back as if she were about to pour it over him all over again.

"Put that thing down," he barked as if it were the most dangerous weapon ever.

She bit down a smile.

"Everything is sticky," he complained. The ratafia had dribbled into his hair, into his ears, and down his neck.

"You may have to go home to change." Lu was not at all chagrined at the thought of him having to leave.

"I recognise you. You are that lady from the library." He narrowed his eyes. "You did this on purpose."

"Me? No! You are no gentleman to suggest this. It was an accident. Like I said. I stumbled. I am so very sorry for it." The lie came glibly over her lips. "Does it burn terribly?" She held out a handkerchief.

He snatched it and wiped his face with it. "What do you think? It's liquor. Of course it burns when you pour it into your eyes." He glared at her with slightly reddened eyes.

"Oh dear." Her tone did not sound at all repentant. "I am certain you will recover in no time. My Great Aunt Mildred tends to say that nothing is more salubrious for the eyes than a good eye bath. It is said to cure all sorts of ailments."

"Surely she doesn't use alcohol to bathe her eyes?" he asked with a satiric undertone.

Lu thought. "She does use Dr Rothely's Elixir, which, I believe, may have a tiny modicum of alcohol in it."

He stared at her. "You are funning. You do know that Dr Rothely is a quack, don't you? And she pours that stuff into her eyes? Your aunt must be mad." He paused. "The thought occurs to me that you might be as well."

Lu felt another rush of anger. "You may be entirely right. It must run in the family. We Windmere women are all stark raving mad. We tend to run around in deserted libraries during balls and attack sleeping men with ratafia." She clasped her hand over her mouth. She hadn't intended to tell him her name at all.

"Windmere, eh?" He looked her up and down. "I seem to recall you have a peculiar sense of humour in addition to a taste for indecent books." He grinned. "Or was it the aunt who has an unconventional taste for, erm, vulgar books? So, you're a Windmere?"

She coloured fiercely. "It's a different aunt. I have two."

"Ah. So you do." He finished wiping his brow, looked at the wet handkerchief thoughtfully, then folded it and pocketed it. "I suppose it is ungentlemanly to return the sticky and soppy item."

Lu felt oddly better after her petty action of revenge. Not that it had been a monumental sort of act, but something in her felt lighter. Almost cheerful. It wasn't nearly enough for those terrible words he'd said a decade ago, which no doubt he'd forgotten since that night he'd been thoroughly foxed. But she'd felt, at least in part, vindicated.

He leaned back on the sofa, crossed his legs, and looked up at her, his eyes narrowed to two slits of ice. She felt the old sense of self-consciousness and shyness engulf her like a cloak. There it was again. The assessment in the eyes. The judgment. The inevitable conclusion of "All Windmere women are beautiful but you...alas..." Of course, no one would say so directly to her face. He did think her homely. He'd said so himself. And he'd also thought she didn't have much in terms of a bosom. Lu involuntarily crossed her arms in front of her chest. He'd also thought kissing her with the eyes open was worth a wager.

Lu flushed scarlet at the memory. She wondered whether he remembered her. Likely not. A man like him, who was perpetually surrounded by women, would not remember a nobody like her. Besides, he'd been too drunk that night. He wouldn't remember that prank, one of many, as she'd been one woman of many whose prospects he'd ruined.

"The Windmere family is confoundingly large," he said.

Lu shrugged. She started to feel uncomfortably aware that she was alone with him in the library. Her aunt would look for her. If they found her together with St Addington ... she shuddered. Being found alone with him here meant not only certain ruin, but also that her season was over before it had even started. For one short moment, she considered it. The scandal would be profound, but then she could return to Bath and be left in peace...

...it was nonsense, of course. She couldn't do this to Jessica.

Lu came to a resolution. She was determined not to cringe any longer. Not to be ashamed anymore. She pulled herself up proudly. "Yes, my family is confoundingly large. I am Lady Ludmilla Windmere. The former Duke of Amberley's daughter."

He shot her an alert look. "You are Lady Ernestina Rutherford's ward?"

"I am her niece."

He knit his forehead together. "You are Hector's cousin, then."

"You know him?"

He shrugged. "Eton."

Her aunt, indeed, had mentioned that.

"Why are you sleeping in the library in the middle of a ball?"

"Why are you skulking about the library shelves in the middle of a ball, pouring ratafia over hapless gentlemen, instead of dancing?" he countered.

She shrugged. "Sometimes I prefer the company of books over people. As for the other thing, I did explain it was an accident."

"Ah yes. Understandable. Wanting to prefer the company of books over people, I mean. As for the accident—"

"And you? Why are you here?" she interrupted him.

"To escape the matchmaking mamas, of course." He threw a nervous look at the door. "They are forevermore at my heels."

Lu nodded. "Understandable. I suppose it must be quite terrifying to be surrounded by women who perpetually want to drag one to the altar."

"You have fairly nailed the issue." He folded his arms. "It seems we do understand each other."

"In a manner."

She met his ice-blue eyes. Something went through her veins, something intense the flared up at the depths of her being. Mesmerised, Lu was unable to tear her eyes away.

The words were on her lips. *Was it you? Are you*

Addy? Are you the one with whom I have been corresponding all this time?

She opened her lips.

Voices approached, rapidly, coming closer.

"Zounds!" Lu looked at the door in alarm. If anyone were to find her here, all alone with the wicked viscount, it was inconceivable what would happen. The scandal! Her reputation! Her aunt...it was the thought of her aunt, mainly, that instigated her into action.

She stumbled backwards, fluttered about in a circle, and finally scrambled behind the brocade curtains.

St Addington, of similar frame of mind, shot up, jumped with one leap over the table and dove after her. Just in time, for at that moment, the door opened.

"....in here. Look, I told you no one would be here," said a high, lisping female voice. "They're all dancing the quadrille."

Lu frowned and looked at St Addington, who frowned back.

Lu had the ridiculous desire to giggle. She bit hard on her bottom lip. He placed a long finger on his lips.

"Oh, how unhappy I am," the lisping voice continued. "What shall we do?"

"Dearest, dearest heart. How I have pined. How I have yearned!"

Lu's eyes widened.

"There is only one thing to do, dash it all. Marry me."

St Addington rolled his eyes.

"You know I can't. I am supposed to marry Standish."

"That blackguard! He doesn't deserve you. He doesn't appreciate you! You deserve to be carried always, so your tiny, dainty-wainty feetsies never touch a mere pebble," he said.

Lu desperately pressed her lips together. The muscles in her cheeks twitched.

St Addington's shoulders shook.

"Oh, would you?" the voice sighed.

"Would I what?"

"Carry me always so my tiny, dainty-wainty feet never touch the ground."

Lu's overbrimming eyes met St Addington's. She would have exploded in uninhibited laughter if St Addington hadn't had the presence of mind to clasp his hand over her trembling lips.

"What shall we do, oh what shall we do?"

"Let us elope."

"But how?"

"At midnight."

"Like Cinderella! I shall wear my ball gown."

"Dash it, no, a regular plain gown so we don't attract any attention."

"I will wear my dancing slippers, then. I shall lose them so you can carry me."

Lu was dying. Tears ran down her face.

"Confound it no, won't work. Tomorrow is the race. I have placed too high a bet on it. Dearest heart, we can elope after that."

"You love your horses more than me." The lady sounded sulky.

"I do not, dearest heart, I swear. Let me prove it to you."

A sound of a smacking kiss.

The lady sighed.

Lu stilled.

St Addington's eyes glinted sardonically.

"There. Do you believe me now?"

"Oh, yes. Let us elope after the race then. What will Mama say?"

"Hush, no word to anyone. This has to remain a secret."

"How exciting!"

"Promise, dear heart, no word to anyone."

"I promise."

The library was quiet.

St Addington dropped his hand.

She was aware of his breathing, his closeness, his body. She smelled his cologne. A mixture of mint and musk, and something else she could not identify. Her lips still tingled from the warmth of his hand on them. Lu's eyes were huge and stared into his. Her heart jolted and her heart pulsed, and she was certain he could hear every hectic beat in the quietness of the library. Goodness, his eyes were of the most startling blue-green she'd ever seen, with golden flecks around the irises. They widened in surprise. He blinked once, twice, as if waking from a trance.

Then he lifted a finger and pulled the curtain gently aside. "That was close. You nearly betrayed us there," he observed, as they stepped out from behind the curtain into the empty library.

"I couldn't help it. They were too ridiculous." She burst into laughter at the memory of the lisping voice.

There was another noise in the hallway, and she

jumped. "I'd better return before someone else comes. Aunt Ernestina will be missing me."

St Addington opened the door slowly and peeked out. "It's safe. I will follow in several minutes."

He flashed her another one of his charming smiles.

Lu stumbled.

Chapter Twelve

Lu RETURNED TO THE BALLROOM, WHICH SEEMED even more stuffed, hot, and frenzied than before.

Her aunt was fanning herself vigorously. There was a sheen of sweat covering her ample décolleté. "There you are, child. Where have you been? Never mind. The quadrille is about to begin, and young Marling slipped through my fingers. He is dancing with Miss Susan Starless, now."

"That is fine, Aunt. I will sit here and rest. I am quite fatigued. Besides, you ought not bully the gentlemen to dance with me." Her dance card was quite empty and would remain so until the ball was over. Lu plopped down into her usual seat by the wall, next to the other ladies who were not fortunate to gain a partner in dance. She felt comfortable there. Jessica was dancing with Lord Sainsbury. They made a handsome pair.

"Would you look at that," Aunt Ernestina suddenly muttered.

"What?"

"I don't know how she did it, but she just snagged St Addington."

"Who?" Lu stretched her neck but could not identify St Addington in the crowd. Was he dancing with a ratafia-drenched coat? A slight pang of guilt shot through her, but she quenched it quickly.

"Miss Philippa Peddleton." Aunt Ernestina sniffed. "A nobody."

Then she saw him. Lu had no idea how he'd done it, for he'd changed into a wine-coloured coat, and his shirt was crisp as though freshly laundered. She briefly wondered whether he always took a second set of clothes with him to every ball. Then she saw that he danced with a tall, brunette girl with healthy teeth, because she kept flashing her teeth at him as she smiled.

Lu disliked her instantly. This threw her into some confusion because Lu never disliked anyone. What was wrong with her?

And he, tall as he was, danced quite gracefully. Lu could not tear her eyes away from the couple.

At the end of the dance, Aunt Ernestina beckoned him with one finger.

He saw her, raised an eyebrow, and made a small bow in their direction.

"Aunt, what are you doing," Lu hissed.

"Trust me," she replied smugly.

St Addington made his way over to them.

"Lady Rutherford." He bowed over her hand.

"St Addington, you rascal." She touched his arm with her fan flirtatiously. "It's been a while since we last talked. This is my niece, Lady Ludmilla Windmere."

He bowed over her hand quite formally, as if they'd never seen each other before.

Lu curtsied and kept her eyes fixed on his silver waistcoat. It was most definitely a different kind of waistcoat from the one he'd worn before.

"I haven't seen Hector. Is he here as well?" she heard him ask.

"Hector is in the country with his wife but arriving tomorrow. I wanted to inform you that we are expecting you for supper Saturday night." She rapped her fan on his arm.

That was more of an order than an invitation.

"It will be a pleasure." He bowed.

"In the meantime, children, dance." She gave Lu a small push, so she tumbled into his arms.

"Aunt!" Blushing fiercely, she untangled herself.

"May I ask for this dance?"

She looked up into his laughing eyes.

Dear heaven, it was a waltz. How was she supposed to survive that?

Despite her consistent lack of partners, Lu was a good dancer because she was light on her feet and had a good sense of rhythm, but with St Addington, she had problems concentrating. She felt the eyes of the entire *ton* upon them on the dance floor. More than one matron lifted her lorgnette as they danced by. Indeed, there were whispers and jealous glances, mainly from the women. Lu wished she were anywhere else but dancing with him. Especially when he radiated this warmth and smelled so nice.

Mint and musk.

A delicious combination.

"I am so sorry," she babbled.

"For pouring ratafia all over me?" He did not pull a muscle in his face.

"No. I mean, it was an accident. How often do I have to repeat it?"

"You can protest all you like. I know you did it on purpose."

"You really are quite odious, you know? I meant I am sorry because of my aunt. She can be a force of nature sometimes."

"I know. I've known her since Hector and I were boys."

Lu narrowed her eyes at him, remembering that he'd been good friends with Matthew as well. She wondered whether he remembered that particular incident, and if not, whether she should remind him of it.

"You are scowling. What have I done to incur your wrath?" he asked in a flirtatious tone, which made her scowl even more.

"I suppose I'd rather not be dancing," she said as he twirled her in a perfect curve. "But I am starting to understand the way my aunt's mind works. Dancing with you, I mean. It is an odd kind of paradox that, on one hand, it is a good thing for others to see that the plain Lady Ludmilla is no wallflower. Behold her dancing with a viscount, you know. But on the other hand, if we were to be seen in each other's company for too long, or dance a second dance, heaven forbid, it would result in scandal. People and the rules of society are so very odd, don't you agree?"

St Addington understood immediately. "On account of my very wicked reputation, you mean," he looked down on her through hooded eyes.

"Well, those are your words. One would have to live behind the moon not to know about that."

"Your candour is refreshing. But you are wrong on one account."

"Am I?"

"You are not at all plain."

Lu snorted. "Of course you'd say that."

"And why, Lady Ludmilla, would you say this? Do you not believe that I am being honest?"

"No. You are being one of two things. One: you are being naturally flirtatious, ergo I need not take your compliments seriously. Two: You are being contrary for the sake of being contrary, because I noticed that this is what you like to do. If I'd said my aunt's dress is blue, you'd say no, it's pink."

He looked at her in mock outrage. "I must protest. Granted, I may have a shocking sense of colour, especially when it comes to fashion, but I am certainly not that colour blind! What do you say to my new wine-red coat, by the by? I could not make up my mind whether to wear the wine red or the dark blue one, so I took both along, which has turned out to be a most fortuitous decision, especially after your pernicious atta—I mean, accident. But I digress. As for your second reproach, I must say, you are painting me in the darkest, most ungentlemanly colours, indeed. A true gentleman always agrees with a lady."

Lu snorted. "You are disagreeing with me as we speak."

His eyes laughed down on her. "I know what you will say next. I am not a gentleman, am I right?"

Lu flushed. "Let us change the topic and talk about something more interesting. Who do you think was the couple in the library?"

"Does the topic embarrass you? I was being honest. But very well. I believe the man may have been Lord Eustachius Stilton. I have no idea about the lady. I haven't had the fortune to meet her."

Lu frowned. "She is probably Lady Cynthia Vanheal. I recognized that babyish voice of hers with the lisp. Do you think we ought to be doing something about them?"

He looked down on her. "Do you want to meddle in their affairs?"

"Well. They did talk about eloping."

"So?"

"So?" Her head snapped up. "The lady's reputation will be ruined beyond repair."

He managed to shrug while performing a full turn. "Since she is a willing participant in the whole affair, I fail to see what the problem is."

"Thus speaks the rake," Lu mumbled. The next moment, she could have swallowed her tongue.

"Precisely." There was this icy glint in his eyes again.

"I didn't quite mean that the way it sounded," she said hastily. "I apologize."

"No need to apologize. It is but the truth. We have our wicked ways, we rakes." He bent down to murmur.

"It is commonly known that I tend to seduce women on the ballroom floor, you know."

"Now you're making fun of me. I suppose I deserved that."

"But of course."

Lu thought. "Though I daresay all this talk about your wicked reputation and so forth is probably just rumours. Oh. I know! You probably encourage them, too, don't you? The rumours. It is a calculated ruse. To keep the matchmaking mamas at bay."

He whispered into her ears, wickedly. "Do you care to find out?"

She stomped on his foot.

"Now you stepped on my dainty-wainty feetsies," he complained.

Lu couldn't help herself. She burst out laughing.

SHE WAS STILL LAUGHING in the carriage on the way home.

Aunt Ernestina shook her head.

"What is wrong with her, aunt?" Jessica grabbed one of Lu's hands and patted it to calm her down. "She's been laughing the entire time. It doesn't seem normal."

"'Tis the relieved laughter of a spinster who has danced a waltz with one of the season's most eligible bachelors. He has danced with only two women. That Peddleton woman, but she doesn't count, and our Ludmilla here." She leaned back with a smile. "I am most satisfied with tonight's evening. This ball has been a marvellous success. First, the Prince Regent has singled you out, Jessica. I was right and the gentlemen afterwards scrambled for your hand, didn't they? Now, word will get round that St Addington's danced with Ludmilla, and at the next ball, the men will fall over themselves to secure Ludmilla's hand. I can hear the sweet trumpets of victory. An entire chorus of angels is singing. Oh! The triumph! Well done, girls. Oh, well done."

Lu and Jessica looked at each other, startled.

Lu burst into laughter again.

Chapter Thirteen

St Addington was pondering on the mystery of Lady Ludmilla Windmere as he walked through the streets of London. He liked to stroll home after his clubs and balls, to let the fresh night air clear his mind. A brisk walk helped him think.

He hadn't been entirely sure, until now. After the meeting in the circulating library the other day, he'd had the niggling suspicion that he'd seen her before, that she looked somehow familiar. After the incident today (confound it, what had that been all about?), and the waltz, he was certain.

He had met her before.

But where? And when?

That was, of course, a dilemma he had quite often, that a woman looked familiar, and he couldn't immediately place her. He'd once called an opera dancer Belinda, when her name had been Cecilia, and she'd given him a round slap in the face. Cecilia had been that other girl, confound it if he hadn't already forgotten her face. How could one keep those faces and names apart when most of them looked so similar? The same kind of bonnet, the same kind of hairstyle. Bah.

But she was a slight thing. She gave the impression of wanting to disappear into the wallpaper or furniture, as if she dreaded being noticed. Her hair was black, short, and wispy, and it framed her finely boned face. She had a habit of tilting her head sideways and looking at him as if she were a sparrow. No, she wasn't beautiful. But neither was she ugly or, as she'd called herself, plain. He considered her arresting. She had big, brown, intelligent eyes that reflected every single emotion that went through her. He wondered whether she knew about that. Within a moment, she went from thoughtful, to shy, to humorous— to angry. Blazingly, blisteringly angry. Did she know she looked almost beautiful when her eyes sparkled with anger?

Confound it, he'd seen her before.

A fleeting expression that had lasted but a second. Something stricken in her eyes, something deeply hurt. Reproachful.

He shifted uncomfortably as he raked his memory.

But where? But when?

It hadn't been recent.

The vision of a slim figure in white, waif-like, drifted up from the depths of his memory. An innocent. Almost a child. Huge, dark eyes, full of hurt, shock and reproach as they met his.

St Addington stopped in the street and cursed loudly as it hit him full blast.

The devil! She wasn't *that* girl? Matthew's rich heiress who was to save him from the moneylenders?

What had been her name again? Some duke's daughter. She may very well have been a Windmere.

He groaned out loud.

It was so long ago, he'd forgotten all about it until now. He'd forgotten entirely what the precise circumstances had been—it had been at that cursed Whittlesborough ball as well, hadn't it? Had he challenged Matthew to a bet? They'd tended to do that, he and his friends, especially when they were young and foolish and reckless and drunk. Betting on everything under the moon was how they'd liked to spend their time. It was the thing to do. They'd placed wagers on things as silly as how many flies crashed against the window-pane. Or how many gentlemen collapsed in drunken stupor in front of the doorstep of their club (he'd won that one).

St Addington racked his brain. He may have challenged Matthew to a bet as to whether he had the courage to kiss the girl. He couldn't recall his precise words. He winced. Yes, it had been a stupid thing to do. Callous, even. To him, it had been a wager like any other. Yet it could've ruined her reputation. At that time, he'd thought nothing of it. Then he'd looked up, and there she stood. What the deuce was she even doing there?

She'd given him a look so full of reproach and hurt that it had shot through his entire system, and he'd sobered up instantly, even though he'd been roaringly drunk. He knew on the spot she'd heard every word. He also knew he'd deeply wounded an innocent.

He instantly regretted his words. He wondered

whether to let Matthew know that she was standing right behind him, for the idiot had gone blithely on and on about the bet, and how he wanted to marry the girl only for her dowry, for she was too ugly for his taste. He himself may have goaded him on. Adrian winced.

She'd heard every single word.

He was about to tell Matthew to shut up, when the girl whirled around and disappeared out of their lives.

He'd never seen her again.

Neither had Matthew.

Matthew had been vaguely disgruntled after his heiress had disappeared into thin air. He'd never bothered to tell him that his elected fiancée had overheard them and discovered that he only fancied her for her money. He did not want to get involved, it was none of his business, after all. Matthew had no broken heart. He'd immediately turned to Miss Evelyn Sconderby, the daughter of a baron, whose pockets were heavily plump as well. He'd married her within a month and moved to Bristol. That was the last thing he'd heard about his former crony. He'd forgotten the entire incident until now.

Cursing, St Addington stalked down the road. Of all the deuced, unfortunate, ill-starred coincidences. No wonder she'd poured ratafia down his eyes. He should count himself lucky, for she could've used brandy or whisky. No wonder she'd still been blazingly angry at the waltz. She hadn't been angry at their first meeting, at the circulating library, however. She'd seemed more dazed, and adorably confused as she kept looking through the window. What had that been all about?

"Fool, fool, fool," St Addington muttered. He felt like dashing his brains against the wall.

When he looked up, he recognised the house where he stood.

His legs had automatically taken him to Covent Garden, to one specific house.

"Excellent," he muttered, as he stepped up to the door and lifted the brass knocker.

He badly needed some distraction.

Chapter Fourteen

DEAR ADDY,

Lu wrote. Then stopped, as she stared into space with a vapid smile on her face, recalling the events of the previous night.

She shook her head.

Addy.

She wanted to write to Addy.

Looking down on the paper, she frowned. Something happened that she'd never thought was possible before. She didn't know what to tell him.

What should she tell him?

Her thoughts drifted to St Addington again. Should she just ask him outright and in person? He was coming for supper in two nights. She imagined asking him over the *foie gras*: "Oh, by-the-by. Is there a certain Addy living with you in the same house? He likes to write letters."

To which he could reply in three ways:

1. Never heard of the fellow.

2. Yes, he's my under butler.

3. You're looking right at him, dear.

Numbers one and two were problematic. Because they were bound to be followed by follow-up questions. "No. Who the devil is he?" or "Yes. He's my under butler. Why are you familiar with my domestics?" Then she'd be in the suds. She'd have to confess to their inappropriate correspondence, and that just wouldn't do.

Number 3 would be an unmitigated disaster. If people were to find out she'd been secretly corresponding with London's most eligible bachelor—who also happened to be the scandalous viscount—that would mean the end of her reputation. The scandal!

Their aunt would force them to get married.

She shuddered. One thing she was certain: she would never, ever marry him. She'd seen him at his play. She'd seen him at his worst. She'd seen what he was capable of. St Addington was every bit as callous and cruel as his reputation painted him to be. He could ruin a girl's life in an instant. As he had ruined hers.

Though to be fair: it had been Matthew, really, whom he'd unveiled. If at all, she should be angry at Matthew and grateful to St Addington. It hadn't been St Addington's fault that Matthew had revealed himself to be a fortune hunter...but somehow, it was easier to blame it all on him.

Deep down, Lu knew she was being unfair by using him as a scapegoat.

Lu threw down her quill with a sigh. The ink splattered on the paper. Now, she'd have to start all over again.

She was so confused!

The mere thought of St Addington being Addy made her mouth dry up and her stomach flutter. Lu knit her forehead into a frown and wondered what to do about it. She was a coward for letting things go on as they did. She should be an adult about it and confront him. Instead of keeping up the charade, and keep on playing this hide and seek, she should call him out on it.

Let him call on her. Like regular people normally tend to do. What on earth was the problem?

She picked up her quill again with a thudding heart. For the first time, she would sign: Lady Ludmilla Windmere, Rutherford House, Grosvenor Square, London. She would be straightforward with her identity and her address.

Then he would come calling the very next day.

They'd drink tea and converse politely in her aunt's drawing room.

The mere thought gave her anxiety.

Why on earth was she so resistant to it?

Lu shook her head, stumped.

She threw the quill down, crumpled the paper into a ball, pushed back the chair and got dressed for dinner.

Coward, she scolded herself.

Coward.

Chapter Fifteen

Lu would have liked to put on her old, grey-chequered dress for the supper party, with her mud-coloured shawl. It was safe. She'd feel plain and invisible in it. But Aunt Ernestina would have none of it.

"Put on the sage green satin," she ordered.

It was a lovely gown. It had a white lace over-gown and trimming on the bottom. Together with a light shawl and some pearls, she thought she no longer looked like her staid old spinsterish self.

Her cheeks were naturally red (from all the nervous excitement, no doubt) and her brown eyes looked soft and dreamy.

"You look positively pretty," Jessica exclaimed when she saw her. "You have the Windmere beauty after all. Just differently. It comes through at the second glance."

"Oh, piffle, Jessica. But thank you anyway. It is nice of you to say so."

Jessica herself was a gorgeous vision in white lace and pink satin. Her cheeks were pink, too, and her eyes sparkled with excitement. It occurred to Lu that there'd been this sense of excitement about Jessica for quite a while already. She'd said she was in love, hadn't she? Lu wondered who it was. She hadn't noticed any preferential treatment towards any of the gentlemen she'd danced with at the ball. She seemed to treat all gentlemen with the same kind of sweet but aloof courtesy. Lu made a mental note to talk to her later.

In the meantime, Lu's foot would not hold still. It kept tapping on the floor. When she tried to force her foot to remain still, her fingers started tapping on the tabletop. She found the room to be hot and took off her shawl. Then she suddenly felt too exposed, and she draped the shawl over her décolleté again. Dear me, it was only a supper party. Why this nervousness?

Because she hated socialising, of course.

He was coming, too. Lu wasn't entirely certain whether his acceptance of her aunt's invitation had been mere lip service, or whether he really was coming. She had not dared ask her aunt.

At any rate, Aunt Ernestina's small dinner party turned out to be a glamorous affair.

Cousin Hector, the current Duke of Amberley, had arrived earlier, together with his wife Miranda, as well as all remaining Windmeres, too many to count. Aunt Ernestina must have invited most lords, ladies, dukes, and earls of the realm.

Hector had taken Lu's hand into his sweaty one and said stuffily that she was welcome in his home. Any time. Lu had felt tempted to reply that he'd been overheard saying he did not want a pair of spinsters in his house and anyway, Whistlethorpe Hall had been her home before her father died, which she'd been forced to leave thanks to him. But never mind. This was the way things were done, after all. She'd bitten on her tongue and forced herself to smile so her face cramped and turned to Miranda.

Lu normally liked Miranda. She was a bit of a vapid thing, and as she listened to her chatter, Lu realised with sinking heart that Miranda was telling her in detail about all the changes they were making in her—pardon—*their* home.

"We are tearing down the folly in the lake, ugly old thing, and building a bridge over the lake instead." She motioned her hands as if modelling it out of the air.

The Folly on Magic Island. It had been her favourite childhood place. It had been her secret hideaway when she wanted to get away from people. One could only reach it by rowing a boat across to the island. The folly wasn't new, agreed; it was halfway covered with moss and really looked like the ruin it attempted to imitate. It'd been built by her grandfather for her grandmother, on their twentieth wedding anniversary. They'd been deeply in love. Lu had liked to hide among the ruins, reading books, eating biscuits, and generally, just daydreaming and whiling her time away. And now, Miranda said they would tear it down and build a bridge across the little lake.

Lu felt like bursting into tears. Instead, she ground her teeth and nodded with a fixed smile on her face.

"I am also having the drawing rooms refurbished. And the Chinese room as well. It is hideously ugly, so I will have all the odd Chinese furniture and vases stored away and turn it into a drawing room."

"But Whistlethorpe Hall already has ten drawing rooms," Lu couldn't help but point out. Why would she want an eleventh?

"Yes, but they are in all sorts of dark, dreary colours. I like it bright and colourful and happy. Bright mauve. Don't you think it's such a lovely colour, Cousin? It is the newest rage, you know. Imagine everything in mauve, the walls matching the sofas and the carpets and the curtains. With magnolia prints as well. It will be my very own personal space. My very own, mauve drawing room."

Mauve! Goodness. Miranda was right that the Chinese room was more of a museum than anything else, since it harboured all the odd bits and pieces, vases, furniture, paintings, and masks that her grandfather had brought from his trips to the Far East. It had been one of her favourite rooms, and she'd personally dusted the items in there, never letting a servant touch anything. What would Miranda do with all the precious memorabilia? Banish it to the attic? Did she even know how valuable that Ming vase was? Or the Korean Celadon bowl? One could howl with frustration. Once more, she had to bite her tongue hard. She felt the coppery taste of blood fill her mouth.

Lu swallowed.

Her home was no longer her home, she kept reminding herself, and Miranda as the new Duchess of Amberley had every right to do whatever she wanted. Even painting all the rooms mauve, purple and pink, with yellow dots. But oh, how her heart—and her tongue —bled!

The guests arrived one by one, and with her spirits already dampened, the old anxiety befell Lu. There were too many people in the room. The air was too heavy. Too many glances were thrown her way, curiously, noticing her.

She could get out of it with an excuse. She could retreat, saying she had a terrible migraine. It was partially true. But the door opened once more, and more guests arrived. How they were all going to fit into the dining room was a mystery to her. With a sigh, Lu braced herself.

"St Addington, old scum. Good to see your ugly face." Hector pounded St Addington's back with enthusiasm. He pounded Hector right back with equal force.

"Amberley, you scallywag. I see your hideous grimace hasn't changed. It's good to be here."

Men do have an odd way of showing their affection for each other, Lu thought.

He kissed Miranda's hand, who simpered.

Then he turned to Aunt Ernestina. "Lady Rutherford. You are the most beautiful woman in the room," he murmured over her hand.

"And you are the biggest rogue in England. Turn your deadly charm to those who appreciate it."

"You wound me to the quick." He placed a hand over his heart and smiled.

"Scoundrel." Aunt Ernestina fluttered her eyelashes at him.

Aunt Ernestina. Fluttered. Her. Eyelashes.

Lu gaped.

Then he turned to her. And she knew she was in trouble.

"Lady Ludmilla."

He must have kissed her hand, for it tingled, and she must have curtsied, because that was what she was taught to do.

But beyond that, her brains seemed to have turned to mush, and all her bones had melted. She stammered something; his lips curled to a smile.

"I am glad to see your aunt has banished all the ratafia. Must I brace for a champagne attack instead?" he murmured into her ear.

"Of course not," she stammered. Somehow, all wit had left her.

At lunch, she regained her composure somewhat.

It happened over the pudding.

The footmen served syllabub in crystal glasses.

Lu spooned her syllabub with concentration.

She'd wanted to ask him a very important question, and now the time had come. He sat across from her, flirting with his table partner, Lady Barington, who was at least twice his age but who flirted like there was no tomorrow. It would have amused Lu to no end if she hadn't worried so much about the upcoming question she was about to ask St Addington.

They were talking about the newest play on Drury Lane. With thumping heart, Lu waited for a lull in the conversation so she could pose her question.

She ran her tongue over her lips.

Then Hector bellowed from across the table. "Say, St

Addington, how come Addy's not here with us tonight? I am certain he's been invited. Hasn't he, Aunt?"

Lu dropped her spoon with a clank.

"Of course he has. But he has declined. He wasn't at the Whittlesborough ball, either." her aunt observed. "Most unaccommodating of him not to have come. I have had to rearrange the entire seating arrangement because of him."

"My cousin is unfortunately indisposed," St Addington lowered the glass with Madeira.

"How terrible. What ails the poor man?" Lady Barington's voice was full of concern, yet fluttered her eyelashes at St Addington as she turned to him.

St Addington shrugged. "He has a fever. I daresay it's the influenza."

"Oh, I know just the thing to cure influenza. Dr Rothely's Elixir. Has he tried it?"

"Dr Rothely's commonly known to be a quack," her aunt interjected. "Tell Addy not to try it, St Addington. Rest is all he needs."

Lu choked on the syllabub.

"Say, Lady Ludmilla, are you quite well?" St Addington asked.

Lu couldn't stop coughing. She drank from her water glass, and downed it with one gulp.

Conversation continued with Lady Barington rattling off a long list of cures against influenza, which included Dr Bateman's Pectoral drops as well as an Oriental Vegetable Cordial.

"You have a cousin named—Addy?" Lu asked St Addington so abruptly that he looked taken aback.

"But yes. Adam Adey."

"Has he been living with you in Bruton Street for long?"

St Addington took a sip of his red wine. "About three years."

Three years. For as long as they've been writing to each other.

Adam Adey.

Addy.

His cousin.

Who lived with St Addington in the same house.

She'd got everything wrong.

Chapter Sixteen

Lu sat by the piano, blindly flipping the pages of the Mozart minuet that Jessica had just finished playing so adorably. Lu herself claimed to be an indifferent player, which wasn't true at all. But she loathed performing, so she let everyone know that she was no good at playing. For some reason, everyone believed her.

"You're oddly quiet, Lady Ludmilla," a low voice murmured into her ear. Lu jumped.

St Addington set down his glass of champagne on the piano and sat on the bench next to her. His fingers ran lithely over the piano keys, and he played a cheerful little tune that she did not recognise.

"What is the matter?" he asked.

"Nothing. I am just a bit distracted. Say. Have you been able to confirm that the man in the library was Lord Stilton?"

"No. I am not so sure it interests me, either. I am more interested in—" He fixed his gaze on her, and once more she felt a melting sensation.

"In?" she asked, breathless.

"In what is in front of me. Right now." He spoke in his casual, jesting way.

"Wha—what is that?"

He picked up his champagne glass, held it up, took a sip and met her eyes over the glass rim.

What a dreadful flirt he was!

"That is my aunt's best champagne. I will tell her that you liked it."

There was laughter in his eyes.

Somehow, knowing that he wasn't Addy simultaneously disappointed and relieved her. With the relief being more dominant. In fact, she felt her self-consciousness fall away. He was just a rake, and it didn't matter whether he flirted with her or not. He was used to flirting. He'd even flirted with Jessica, making her blush, and that was quite something because she was used to men's flirtations.

He wasn't Addy. Ergo, it didn't matter whatsoever what he thought of her. She already knew he thought of her as that homely Windmere girl.

She found she no longer cared.

As he leaned with one arm against the piano, she studied his face. He had deep-set eyes. His eyebrows were odd, very light, almost white, the nose strong, the lips curved prettily, almost womanly. Golden curls tumbled over his forehead. His chin was strong, and there was the tiniest of dents in the middle. She'd seen a bust of Alexander the Great once in the British museum. St Addington had probably stood as a model, Lu thought.

"Why do you do it?" The words tumbled over Lu's lips without thinking.

"Do what?" He lifted his champagne glass. "Make the prettiest lady in the room, who happens to stand right before me, blush?"

"Oh, do be quiet. Can you set your flirtation aside for one moment? Thank you. I meant exactly that. Pretending like you are incapable of forming two thoughts in your head that do not revolve around flirtation."

"It is a challenge," he conceded. "With all these beautiful women in the room, what else is one to do?"

Lu turned away with an impatient huff.

"Although there are none who are as perceptive and have as much intelligence as you."

Lu stood up.

"Sit down, Lady Ludmilla. I see I offend you with my compliments, even though they are given honestly. Tell me, did you ever get around to reading *The Imaginary Adulteress*?"

Lu pulled a face. She'd read the *Imaginary Adulteress* with gritted teeth, out of principle. It'd been awful, but read it she did. "I did not like it at all. The language is archaic, and one can make neither head nor tail of the plot. I daresay you would enjoy it very much."

"Oh? And why do you think so?"

"Damsels in distress, pirates, slavery, and a hero who dies halfway through the story only to reappear in three different disguises and to be tearfully reunited with the heroine in the end. Her three children, who she thought were from different men, are all really from him." Lu rolled her eyes. "Ergo the title *Imaginary Adulteress*. She never committed adultery. It is a very naughty story."

"Naughty. Excellent. It sounds just the right kind of thing for me, though now you have spoiled the plot for me."

"Come and think of it, you seem to have something in common with the hero. Both of you appear to wear masks."

His eyes glittered. "Indeed?"

"You and the hero seem to share some traits. But you will have to discover this on your own. I will lend you the book, gladly."

He placed a hand over his heart. "It will be an honour to read a book that you have read. In my case, of course, reading means just looking at the pictures."

She uttered a brief laugh. "Of course. Tell me, however. Your cousin, Mr Adey. Does he like to read?"

"Adam? Oh yes. He has his nose in a book day in and day out. He does nothing else but read and write. It is difficult to get him to leave the house. Except for the theatre, for which he has a great passion."

Lu nodded. Of course. Addy not only loved the theatre, but he was also very knowledgeable about drama in general, especially Shakespeare.

"Pray, what does he write? Is he an author?"

St Addington shrugged. "Now that you mention it, I ought to ask him, for he is forevermore scribbling something or other, letters or manuscripts. That rascal. That is probably precisely what he is doing, his big secret. Maybe he is writing a book."

"A book? Oh." That would be just like Addy. "Interesting how your cousin seems to be so different from you in terms of personality."

He narrowed his eyes. "Why this sudden interest in my cousin, I wonder? Have you met?"

She flushed and found nothing to reply to this.

"We are as different as night and day," he said cheerfully. "It may appear odd to you, Lady Ludmilla, but I am uncommonly fond of my cousin. He was the brother I never had. We grew up together, scouring the countryside, falling off trees and into brooks and lakes." He grinned, and for the first time, Lu had the impression that that was the first authentic smile she'd ever seen on his face.

Lu nodded. "Yes. Especially lakes. It is particularly charming if there's a small island to which one can row—"

"To escape the strict history tutor. With an apple or two in a satchel—"

"And a good book—"

"And a fishing rod—"

"One can while away some sunny, pleasant hours in peace and quiet on that island."

They stared at each other.

Lu felt something lodge in her throat. "Until something happens, inevitably that breaks the peace."

"Usually it's the tutor, vile man, who comes scuttling across the meadow, shouting at the top of his lungs. We'd get a good whipping afterwards for having skipped our morning lessons." St Addington winced.

Lu was silent.

"What was it in your case that ended the tranquillity?"

Lu's eyes lifted and went across the room. There he stood. Corpulent, self-satisfied, boisterous, and loud. The new Duke of Amberly was what happened.

St Addington followed the direction of her eyes. "Oh. I see. Of course. I am very sorry. It must have been a terrible shock to you to lose not only your father, but in one fell swoop, your childhood home as well."

"It wasn't a shock, precisely. Father had been ailing, and one had to expect the worst to happen sooner or later." Her voice drifted off. She'd not anticipated the feeling of rootlessness, of falling into a hole without a bottom afterwards.

She'd gone from being the daughter of a duke to a mere nobody, a spinster whom no one wanted. Very well, so maybe she'd been a spinster already prior to her father's death—some voices said she'd been born a spinster—but at least she'd been a spinster with purpose and independence. The loss of status and title did not matter to her, but she missed her life at Whistlethorpe Hall, for she'd been as good as running her father's household, especially in the latter years when he declined more and more. She was good at managing the gigantic house, directing the servants, and at making sure the household ran smoothly. It had been difficult giving all that up.

Now she took care of Mildred and helped in her household as much as she could, but it wasn't quite the same.

Silence stretched between the two, and Lu shifted uncomfortably.

"It took some time to get used to," she eventually said.

"St Addington," Hector boomed from across the

room. "Come here, old man. And tell me about that shocking incident in the theatre the other day."

His eyes were still on hers. He nodded at her and crossed the room to join Hector.

She felt something had shifted.

They'd shared memories. A moment of honesty. Some kind of rapport was there that hadn't been there before. It was like he'd allowed her a tiny glimpse into his soul.

And she liked what she saw.

JESSICA SLIPPED INTO HER ROOM. Lu was sitting in front of her dressing table in her night shift, and her fingers played with the pearl necklace that she was still wearing around her neck.

"Jessica. Did you have a nice evening?"

Jessica bounced on her bed with a huff. "Somehow I'd imagined it all to be different."

"How so? You mean, in general terms, or just tonight?"

"In general. The balls are wonderful. The glamour and glitter. But somehow..." Jessica hesitated. "It seems as though behind all the fawning, there isn't much substance. Regarding the gentlemen, I mean."

Those were some of the most profound words Lu had ever heard Jessica utter.

"Oh, Jessica." Lu got up and took Jessica's hands into her own.

"I know Aunt wants me to find someone to marry, and she said I wouldn't have a problem doing so by the end of the month. You know," Jessica hesitated before she continued, "I am sure she is right. I could smile at any of those fops, and they would come calling tomorrow. And I'd be engaged to them. To a perfect stranger. And then we'd get married. And maybe we'll be desperately unhappy because we don't love each other. And I realised I would rather like to know what that feels like. To be married to someone I love. Lu?"

"What?"

"What do you know about love?"

Lu hesitated.

"I was wondering whether—so long ago, at your last season—whether something had happened that made you turn away from it all. Were you in love?"

Lu clasped Jessica's hand tightly. "I thought I was," she admitted, slowly. "He was very kind, and attentive, and he was the only man who ever asked me to dance. I was always a wallflower, you know."

"Is he someone I know?"

Lu shook her head. "He is long married."

"What happened?"

"It turned out that his kindness and attentiveness were a pretence. He was a fortune hunter trying to win a bet. I overheard him say so to his friends." Lu swallowed. "He wasn't interested in me at all. He thought me ugly and only wanted me for my money."

"Oh, Lu. Oh, Lu!" Tears welled up in Jessica's eyes. "What a horrid man! Good for you that you did not marry him. Why did you never tell me? No wonder you retreated from everything."

Seeing Jessica cry over her made her own tears rise.

Lu dabbed at the corner of her eyes. "It's so long ago, Jessica, and he doesn't mean anything to me now. In fact, I now wonder what I ever saw in him. But I know one thing, what I must have felt for the man was not love. It was probably just infatuation."

Infatuation.

That was it.

"What about the gentleman you told me about, Jessica? The one who saved you?"

She made an impatient gesture. "Like you. Mere infatuation. Nothing ever came of it."

"I am so sorry, Jessica." Lu hugged her, then she got up.

Shortly before she reached the door, Jessica turned around. "What do you think about St Addington? He's so very handsome, isn't he?"

Lu noticed with alarm that there were two hectic spots of red on her cheeks.

"Yes, he is handsome. He is also a terrible rake."

"So they say. Do you believe the rumours to be true?"

"In general, I don't listen to rumours. But one cannot help but wonder: if they are not true, why is St Addington going out of his way to almost prove them to be true?"

"Yes, isn't he? I have thought so myself. I believe he isn't quite the man he likes everyone to believe. He was quite kind to me when he volunteered to flip the pages for me when I played, and we talked a bit afterwards."

"Jessica! Don't tell me that it is St Addington you've fallen in love with?"

Jessica's blush deepened. She hesitated before replying. "Oh no, I wouldn't dream of it, Lu. He's such a rake, isn't he? Not at all the thing."

Lu looked at her with a worried frown. "I hope so. He would only cause you a heartache."

A feeling of disquiet remained after Jessica had left.

What a muddle this was turning into!

Chapter Seventeen

THAT HAD BEEN A COLOSSALLY STRANGE EVENING, ST Addington decided as he returned home.

The butler let him in, and the footman took his hat and stick.

Normally, he still went to the club afterwards. But tonight, he was oddly reluctant to do so. He felt like he had to mentally rethink the events of the evening.

And *her*.

The difference, this time, was that there hadn't been that reserve, that antagonism he'd received from her earlier.

He was certain she would remember his role that fateful night at the ball when he'd challenged Matthew to the bet. Of course she'd remembered him.

But tonight, she'd been elsewhere with her thoughts. Almost absent-minded.

He'd felt his mask slip once or twice. And he was certain she'd seen past it altogether. He wasn't sure how he felt about that.

He'd only ever allowed Adam to do so.

Adam, his cousin, the brother he'd never had. Adam had been the only one who'd continued to believe in him when no one else did.

When his world had tilted and everyone, including his father, had believed the worst of him. His father had gone to the grave believing he was a heartless philanderer and murderer. There was nothing he could've said or done that would've made him believe otherwise. Sometimes, St Addington thought, he had the impression his father preferred to believe this of his only son. As if that gave him some sort of perverse satisfaction. And the rest of society did the same. To blazes with what the rest of society thought. But the fact that his father did so as well had cut him deep.

To this very day, the rumours persisted.

That he'd seduced Lady Holborn and shot her husband. This had marked the beginning of his inglorious career as a rakehell, and many more dastardly deeds were to follow.

He'd been so young, merely seventeen. An innocent still. So very naive. She'd tried her best to seduce him. He still saw her beautiful, painted, cold face, the cold glitter of determination in her eyes. He didn't know how to resist, at first. She'd somehow managed to separate him from his friends, and he found himself in a boudoir, alone with her. She'd slipped out of her dress and stood in front of him in all her naked glory. He'd backed up, horrified, until he felt the curtain behind him.

"There is only one way out." She pulled her painted lips to a calculating smile. "And that is through me."

He'd thought quickly. "Wrong." He turned, pulled the curtain aside and tore the French windows open. He stood on a balcony.

"Foolish boy. You cannot jump. It will be the death of you."

He looked down and gulped. They were three storeys high. There were no bushes on the ground, no flower beds that would feather off the blow.

She advanced, and he backed off.

He climbed over the railing.

"Foolish boy," she whispered, "you would choose death over this?" She pointed with her hand at her beautiful, naked body.

"Any time," he said, turned, and jumped.

Adrian had jumped off many trees in his lifetime. Once, he'd even jumped off the roof of a barn. This was slightly higher. One thing he knew: it all depended on how one landed. It all depended on rolling off.

He tucked in his legs to roll off on the grass, landed sideways and felt his right leg topple underneath with a crack, and a tremendous flash of pain shot through his ankle. At first, he thought he'd broken his leg. But the crack and the pain didn't come from the fall—it came from a bullet. Someone was shooting at him. A bullet had grazed his foot, and he was bleeding.

Up, at the balcony, was a fracas; there was another man with her. He recognised Lord Holborn, who gesticulated wildly as he shouted. Lady Holborn pulled him back, and he wrestled with her. All of a sudden, she gave him a mighty shove, he flailed with his arms and toppled right over the balcony. A second shot went off as he hit the ground with a sickly crack.

Adrian hadn't waited. He'd pulled himself into the bushes, with immeasurable strength; to this day he wondered how he'd managed to do so. He hobbled to the gate, where his carriage waited, and fainted into the arms of his coachman.

The next day, the news was splattered all over the papers that The Honourable Adrian Adey, son and heir of the Viscount St Addington, had ignominiously shot and killed Lord Holborn in the back after he'd seduced Lady Holborn.

"They say I'm a murderer," he'd told his father, white-lipped. His wound had been taken care of by a surgeon, but it still throbbed painfully.

"And so you are," his father had replied coldly. "You are lucky that I have influence with the authorities. I have told them that it was a duel that unfortunately ended in Holborn's demise. I paid them a fortune to let you go." He hadn't believed Adrian when he protested that it had been Lady Holborn. Everyone preferred to believe the worst of him. As had his aunt, and his cousins. The entire clan.

The only person who'd stood by his side had been Adam.

Quiet, bookish Adam, who'd looked at him with his calm, grey eyes and said, "I believe you."

People's behaviour never ceased to baffle him. There were two groups that contradicted each other in the way they treated him: the group of widows and matchmakers who chased after him, for despite his reputation, he was considered a catch on the marriage mart—no doubt because of his title and fortune. And the other group, which consisted of debutantes and damsels who cringed from him, as if his mere presence sullied their reputation —yet they followed his every move once he entered a ballroom, and their eyes were full of desire.

Lady Ludmilla did not belong to either group. That was most refreshing, indeed. In this regard, she was like Adam.

"You have to show them who you really are, Adrian," Adam kept telling Adrian in his quiet, reasonable way.

But how? And why should he?

"People will believe the worst of me anyway, so I might as well embrace it," he'd told Adam and thrown himself into another night of vices.

Embrace the lie and live it as though it were true. That had been the motto of his life.

Ah, but how he was tiring of it all. The only thing that had kept him sane was his weekly assignation in Covent Garden.

Even Adam believed he was visiting a brothel, but that was not so.

He was visiting Edmund Kean, the celebrated actor, who had agreed to tutor him in the art of acting.

He felt himself renewed, reborn, another man altogether when he was on stage. Ah, he'd be an actor if he could, join the travel troupe and tour the country, with nary a care in the world.

What a life that would be.

Chapter Eighteen

DEAR ADDY,

I must apologise for having missed our rendezvous the other day. If you can forgive me, would you care to meet me once more, at the same spot, on Thursday next?

I promise I will be there this time.

Your friend,

Lu

"JESSICA. I need to ask you a favour."

Lu stood in her sister's bedroom and watched as the abigail brushed her sister's hair. Jessica had glossy blonde hair that hung in thick curls down her back. She waited until the maid was done and left the room before she continued to speak.

It was not easy for her. She'd never been particularly close to Jessica due to their age difference, and now she had to reveal her secret to get Jessica to help her.

"You look worried." Jessica got up from her dressing

table. She wore a pretty morning gown in pale green. Lu was back in her old comfortable brown flannel gown. She'd salvaged it from Aunt Ernestina's maid, who was about to give it away. She twisted one end of her scarf around her fingers as she searched for words.

"Let us sit down," she eventually said.

They sat in the group of armchairs by the window, which overlooked Grosvenor Square.

"The thing is this," Lu began. "I don't have very many friends, as you know. So the precious few I do have are very dear to me."

"Poor Lu! All this time alone with Great Aunt Mildred in Bath has fairly turned you into a hermit, while I was amusing myself in London. I do feel guilty about it. We should've stayed together from the very beginning."

"Yes, well, I am here now, so the point is moot. What I wanted to say is—this may sound very unorthodox, improper, even, but I have been maintaining an episto-lary correspondence for over three years. Almost since the day I moved into Great Aunt Mildred's home."

"You have got me all agog now. Epistolary correspon-dence? How is that improper?" Her eyes brightened with interest. "Lu and the word 'improper' can hardly be mentioned in the same sentence, can they?"

"Well, the thing is this." Lu hemmed and hawed. "My friend is a–a–a—"

"Oh! Let me guess! An actress? A famous person, even? Or, wait." Jessica placed her index finger on her lips as she thought. Then she raised it. "The queen herself!"

Lu emitted a startled laugh. "The queen? How on earth would I manage to privately correspond with her?"

"Well then, spit it out! Who is it?" Jessica jumped up and down in excitement.

"I suppose there is no other way to put it. He's a man." She clapped her hands over her mouth as if she'd said something vulgar.

"Ooh! You don't say! Lu! How can you? How positively indecent, indeed! Pray tell me: who is he? Is he someone I know? Is he a gentleman?"

"That's the thing." Lu swallowed. "I'm not sure."

Jessica stared at her. "What do you mean? You don't know whether he is a gentleman? Whether I know him? Or whether you don't know him? But that doesn't make much sense at all."

Lu dropped her head as she whispered, "The latter. I am not sure I know who he really is."

Jessica formed her lips to a round, pink O. "But how can you not be sure? You just said you corresponded with him for over three years?"

Lu pulled at her earlobe, and accidentally undid the hook of the pearl earring she was wearing. She took the pearl drop in her hand and stared at it as if it was the most interesting thing in the room.

"Yes, it does sound odd, doesn't it? But it is the truth. I have my suspicions of who he is. But even so, I keep having doubts." She sighed. "Ultimately, I cannot be certain about his name or his identity until I have proof. And for that, I need your help."

"But Lu, you goose. I don't understand. How is it that you have never met him in all those years?"

"I was living in Bath, and he in London, for one. And until now I was quite content not knowing his real identity, and he mine. For some reason I preferred that he didn't know that I'm a Windmere. But things have changed, and I have sought out his address." She hesitated.

"And?" prompted Jessica.

Lu looked at her in despair. "The man who I saw coming out of the house wasn't at all who I thought he was going to be."

"But Lu. That doesn't mean anything. He may have been a visitor."

"Precisely. Which is why I asked who lived in the house. And it confirmed my suspicion. Only then I discovered I may have been wrong." She placed her hands on her cheeks. "But I am not certain."

Jessica shook her head in confusion. "Am I understanding correctly that you think you know the identity of your epistolary friend? But you keep being unsure about it? And you do not seem ecstatic. Oh! Let me think. In your mind, you've created a prince charming, a tall, dark and handsome sort of man, on a white steed. And he turned out to be fat, short and ugly."

Lu weighed her head back and forth. "Of sorts."

Jessica tore her eyes wide open and stared at Lu. "But Lu! Are you saying you fell in love with him? How wonderful!"

"No!" Lu jumped up. "Absolutely not! I mean, how can one fall in love with someone whose identity one can't be entirely sure of?"

Jessica looked at her, a wise old look in her eyes, like

an owl. "In the end, it doesn't matter what they look like but what kind of rapport one has with them. And I say, you did fall in love! And now you are struggling to adjust to the reality of who he is. But Lu! It really doesn't matter, does it?"

Her sister had it all wrong. Lu decided she'd let her believe what she may.

"Anyway. I need proof. Here is where I would require your help. I would like to set up a meeting to see whether he is the gentleman I believe him to be. The thing is that I don't want to be personally at the meeting."

Jessica folded her arms across her chest with a frown. "You are making less and less sense, my dear sister."

Lu took a big breath. "I am hoping that you would go in my stead."

"Me? But why? He will think I'm you!"

"Precisely."

"He will not actually get to know you at all."

"Exactly."

"And you will not get to know him."

"This is where you're wrong. I will be hiding and seeing him from a distance. And based on that, I can make an educated decision of where exactly this friendship is going, and whether I even want to continue it."

"I take my words back. You don't sound in love at all. You sound calculating."

"Yes, if that is what it takes, so be it. I just need to know who this man is with whom I've been communicating. I want to know it in a safe way, from a distance, without him knowing who I am."

"But why?"

"Because...because. I just want to do it that way. That's all."

"I don't think I will ever fully understand you, Lu. And here I thought I was the unreasonable one in the family."

Lu flushed. "I know it isn't very honest—"

"Honest? You're intentionally deceiving the poor man. And I can tell you why, too."

Lu was exhausted. "Pray tell me, then. Why?"

"Because you are a coward."

That stung.

She was anything but a coward. She was shy. She was reticent. She wasn't too good in society. And she had no idea how to flirt. She did not feel comfortable meeting gentlemen alone. Did that make her a coward?

"First calculating, now a coward. What can I say? You are right that the honest, right thing to do would be just to meet him there and then, but believe me, I have my reasons for doing it in this way. Jessica. I know you will never understand this. You've always been the pretty one in the family. Things have always come easily to you. You've never wanted anything yet never received it, or been told you couldn't have it, could you? People flock to you like moths to the flame. You are that flame. A gorgeous one. When you enter the room, all heads turn. Surely you know that? It is a credit to you that it hasn't ruined your character, for even though you appear to be a featherhead sometimes, I know in reality you are not. You are every bit as sensitive as I am. I know that deep down, you don't care a tuppence for all that attention. You seek authenticity as much as I, just in your own way. We share that."

Jessica's blue eyes suddenly teared up.

Lu continued talking. "Because of this, maybe you can understand that I am the same, but just the other way. I don't care for attention. I don't want to be seen. I feel safe in the shadow, safe being the unknown one. I don't want that friend, who has grown very dear to me, and who has become the best friend I have ever had, to know who I really am. It is safer for me to remain incognito. You said I may have created a prince charming in my mind, and I think you are partially correct. I think my correspondent friend may have done the same. In his mind, I may be a princess. I don't want to see the look of disappointment on his face when I distort his vision, crushing that dream. For if he is who I think it is, it may be better that I remain that fantasy. But if he is not, I have won myself some time to mentally prepare myself for truly stepping out of my shadow—and owning my identity."

"Oh, Lu! I am so sorry if my words were cruel." Jessica threw herself into Lu's arms. "I am so sorry you feel like that. You shouldn't. I also think you have a terrible sense of self-worth. You are so much prettier than you think you are."

Lu shook her head. "It's not just that."

Jessica blew her nose. "I will help you, gladly. I will go as Lady Ludmilla Windmere, and you will watch from a distance as I interact with your correspondent friend. I shall be your accomplice. Tell me, how are we going to do it?"

Lu told her about the meeting place at Hyde Park, the bench in front of the library. She would be waiting inside and observe through the display window how she met Addy.

"But what is his name, Lu? The man I am supposed to meet instead of you, who might or might not be your friend. You never told me his name."

"His name is Mr Adam Adey."

"Adey?" Jessica echoed.

"He is related to the Viscount St Addington. Until recently, I thought Addy was St Addington, can you imagine? Until I learned he might not be." Lu shuddered.

Jessica had paled and clasped her hand over her mouth.

"I know, I know. Do you understand why I need to know for sure? I need to be absolutely certain Addy is Adey."

"Goodness." Jessica smiled brightly. "What a mix-up. Of course I will help you. Gladly."

She gave Lu a tight hug.

Lu hoped she'd done the right thing, involving her sister. What a mix-up, indeed!

Chapter Nineteen

Adam was lying on the sofa in Bruton Street, his legs covered by a rug, around his throat a scarf. He set the letter he was reading aside when St Addington strolled into the room. The black and tan-coloured hound who'd been sleeping in front of the fireplace jumped up and ran to him with a wagging tail and a bark.

"Down, Macbeth," Adam said.

"I see you are better, Cousin." St Addington scratched the dog behind his ears. "You have been much missed at the Whistleborough ball, not to mention the Rutherford supper party."

"You know I don't hold much for those events. And even though I more or less recovered, I did not feel sufficiently well to attend the dinner. And at the night of the Whistleborough ball I was prostrate with fever, if you recall." His voice sounded nasal from a stuffy nose, but otherwise, he seemed to have recovered.

St Addington sat down in a chair. Macbeth settled by his feet. "So you were. It was the same old thing as every year." He gestured at the letter in his lap. "Don't let me deter you from perusing your correspondence."

Adam flushed. "It is nothing."

"How are things developing in that corner? Have you voiced your feelings to the lady in question yet?"

Adam flushed an even darker shade of puce. "Of course not. We are merely friends. It would be quite inappropriate of me to suddenly express my feelings..." His voice petered off.

St Addington watched him with a raised eyebrow.

"What if she does not reciprocate, and I jeopardise our friendship?" Adam blurted out suddenly.

"Take some advice from a hard-core gambler. Pay good heed to my words: Love's a gamble. You have to take a risk to win or lose it all."

"Is that what love is to you? A mere game?"

"Why, yes. The deeper you play, the more likely it is that you win. Whereby you need to ask yourself, do you really want to win? If yes, why?"

"Naturally, I want to win. Who doesn't? But what about you? You seem to play for the sake of it."

"Indeed. I am not invested in winning as much as you. Ultimately, I don't care whether I win or lose. Which is why I play deep. Alas, my rotten luck will have it that I keep on winning." He shrugged. "What do I do with all these women? I can hardly open a harem."

"Has anyone told you lately that you are simply awful?" Adam shook his head and laughed in exasperation. Then he winced. "Ow. When I laugh, my head hurts. I don't believe you are that callous and cold hearted. I sometimes wonder—" he hesitated.

"Yes? Spit it out, Cousin."

"I sometimes wonder whether you'd be the same person if that cursed Lady Holborn hadn't set her cap at you as she did. I find it most difficult not to feel the strongest kind of dislike, almost hatred for the woman, if you think about how she nearly ruined your character. I say nearly. For even though you pretend otherwise, I know it is not so."

St Addington threw him an amused look. "I am touched. I hardly ever think of the woman. She has moved to France, has she not? Last thing I heard was that she seduced a French Count in the Normandie. I am actually quite grateful to her."

"Grateful? How so?"

"Grateful that she gave me the education she did. I burned myself so badly that the lesson will last for a lifetime."

Adam looked at him with concern. "Yes, that is what I meant. She hurt you badly. She changed your entire outlook on life, on the fair sex, on love. If it hadn't been for her, you'd have completed your studies in Cambridge and lived an entirely different lifestyle."

"You may be right. I could be a scholar who writes useless tracts on the classics that no one is interested in reading. Instead, I am a wastrel who spends his free time in the gaming hells of London. And sometimes on stage, performing incognito in second-rate public theatres in minor towns. Lest anyone recognise me."

Adam shook his head. "It is admirable, really. You are acting doubly: you are impersonating the actor Richard Ridley who is acting as what—Shylock? Prospero?"

"Caliban."

"Brilliant. No one had an inkling that it was you. But we are veering off point. The point I was trying to make is that if it hadn't been for that terrible woman, you'd be long married now, living a sedate and secure lifestyle."

"No need to fret, Cousin. I have some shocking news for you."

Adam sat up, draping his blanket over his knees. "Oh, yes? I am all agog to hear that. What is it? Has a new gambling club opened in Pall Mall?"

St Addington hesitated in a manner that was not customary for the normally effervescent man.

"Cousin! Never say you are being shy about revealing this news? It pertains to a woman?"

St Addington laughed, self-conscious. "Me? Never. Though you are right. It does pertain to a woman."

Adam dropped his letter in astonishment. "Now, why would that have never occurred to me?"

"Sarcasm does not suit you, Cousin. Leave that to me."

"Yes, but now I am all agog with curiosity. Tell me."

"I might also be considering marriage." St Addington proceeded to laboriously polish his quizzing glass with his handkerchief, as if it were the most important activity of the day.

Adam struggled visibly. "Behold me speechless."

"A novelty."

"But no. Adrian! You are funning, right?"

St Addington sighed. "Alas, I am not. I am, in all seriousness, considering shackling myself."

"Who is she?"

"I am not ready to reveal that just yet. It might not lead to anything at all."

Adam nodded eagerly. "I understand. Do you love her?"

St Addington laughed harshly. "Love. Of course not. How does Shakespeare put it so aptly? 'Love is merely a madness.' But if I must choose a lady, it would be her. It'd always be her."

"Sounds suspiciously like love to me. It is wonderful news, Cousin. I hope you don't botch it with the lady."

"Botch it? How so?"

"With all your gambling and womanizing and all that. Though to do you credit, I don't think you've been about all this for a while. Your lifestyle has sobered significantly this past year. Maybe longer. I was wondering whether something was afoot. Now I know! I am very happy."

"Don't be too precipitous. The lady in question knows nothing of her luck. Fact of the matter is, she may not be ecstatic at all to discover my interest in her." He mumbled the latter words so that Adam had to bend forward to catch them.

"Do you care to elaborate on that?"

St Addington stared at the tip of his boots. "I have reason to believe her affections may lie with another."

"Am I imagining it, or is the great womanizer sounding somewhat insecure about securing a woman's affection?"

"Yes, mock me. I suppose I deserve it."

"Let me give you some advice, Cousin. Yes, Adam

Adey is about to give advice on the matters of love and romance to his rakehell of a cousin. Mark my words."

"I am all ears."

Adam stared into St Addington's eyes. "Be yourself."

St Addington blinked. "That's it? I'd have expected something more, I don't know. Epic."

"Yes, but that is what you struggle with the most. Be yourself. I daresay, you are fairly terrified to be yourself."

St Addington opened his mouth to reply something sarcastically cutting, but Adam lifted a hand. "You need not say anything at all in response. Those were my words of wisdom. And now, if you excuse me, I think I will go have a nap after all. I am not entirely over the mountain with this illness just yet. Ah, I am glad about these tidings, indeed."

"I will help you to your room. But before you go, there is another matter to discuss. I need your favour in something."

Adam leaned back on the sofa and looked at him with clear, calm eyes. "Anything, Cousin. For you, anything."

Chapter Twenty

Lu FELT AS IF HER ENTIRE STOMACH HAD TURNED into a beehive. She jumped at every noise, looked over her shoulder at every footstep, and in general tried her best to become invisible by hiding between the dark mahogany shelves. She was back in the library she'd previously visited, dressed in one of her newer but less flashy dresses and bonnets. She ensconced herself behind a bookshelf and held an open book in front of her face, over which she peeked to glimpse through the window to the bench outside. She'd been waiting there at the exact same spot when she'd run into St Addington. This time, she vowed, she would discover the truth.

It would be one of two things:

1. St Addington would appear outside. She would, likely, run around in a circle like a panicking chicken.

2. It was St Addington's cousin, Adam Adey. She had no idea whatsoever what she would do then. She supposed she'd been immeasurably relieved.

SHE RAN her tongue over her dried, cracked lips as she peeked over the book she held in her hands.

Her sister Jessica, dressed in a bright pink pelisse with a matching bonnet, looked charming. She threw a look through the glass window, located Lu, and waved at her.

Lu raised her hand to stop her. She was being too obvious; no one was to know that she was inside the library, watching the encounter. She hoped that when it came down to the actual meeting, Jessica would not give her away.

The clock struck three, and no one showed up. Jessica paraded up and down. They'd brought Mary along, just in case, who trailed several feet behind her, and no doubt wondered what on earth the entire thing was about.

What would she do if Addy never showed up?

It was ten minutes past the hour. He'd never replied to her letter—how could he when she'd not left any address? It could very well be that he decided not to come.

That would be vexing, but Lu began to wish more and more that this would be the case. Because then she could call it over on the spot. She would not pursue the matter any longer.

The moment she'd finished thinking the thought, a gentleman stepped up to Jessica.

He was well dressed, blonde-haired and slim.

A sound escaped Lu.

Adam Adey. St Addington's cousin.

Addy.

He was of somewhat slighter build than his cousin,

but equally tall. His hair was cropped where his cousin's curled in the nape, and he did not have his cousin's world-weary air.

And this, Lu decided, was only good.

He pulled his hat, took a step back, as if surprised, then bowed.

Jessica extended her hand, and he kissed it.

He had pretty manners; Lu noted. Her heart thumped heavily.

The two conversed, and she saw Jessica talk to him in an animated manner. He turned his head, and she saw his profile—oh, he was nice! Very, very nice.

Lu clasped her hands. An odd clump of tears lodged in her throat. Her Addy was the nice, kind man she'd always envisioned. Relief flushed through her.

The two talked. And talked. And talked. Lu squirmed impatiently. Then, she saw how he offered Jessica an arm, and she took it. Both crossed the street, trailed after by Mary, and took a stroll in the park.

Well.

That hadn't been agreed upon, had it?

The agreement had been that Jessica talked to him for one, two minutes only, enough for Lu to identify who he was, and then to leave.

Lu struggled with herself. What to do? Stay here until they returned? Run after them? And say what, exactly?

And so, contrary to what she'd originally decided, contrary to every fibre of her being, contrary to her sense of self-preservation, Lu decided she was done being a coward. She fought a last internal battle, went to the door, and pushed it open with shaking fingers, and stepped out. She would introduce herself to Addy. Once and for all. She crossed the street and rushed after them.

"Oh! Here is my sister." Jessica turned, surprised.

Here it was. The moment of truth. Her bonnet was askew, she was breathless, and out of sorts.

"How do you do." She ran her tongue over her dry lips. "My name is Lady Ludmilla Windmere." She took a big breath and added, "Lu."

Addy's warm grey eyes widened in surprise. "Oh! I thought that—" His eyes went over to Jessica, who looked at him ruefully.

"I am afraid there was a confusion, and you may have mistaken me for my sister. Lu, this is Adam Adey."

He bent over her hand. Lu noted that he was pale, as though he spent a lot of his time indoors. He was an affable, amiable man with an open countenance. He looked from her to Jessica and back. Poor man. He was clearly confused.

"I wrote the letters," she explained. There it was: the moment she'd so dreaded. She held her breath.

"So you did." A vague flush covered his cheeks, and he cast her a shy smile. "Lu. We meet. Finally."

He grasped her hand again as if he did not want to let her go.

Her own mind in a whirl, she wondered what they should do now. Her tongue was tied into a knot, and she could not, for the life of her, come up with anything intelligent to say. Jessica, however, had lots to chatter about. She was usually full of energy, but today she sizzled with a vibrancy that was most unusual. She was chattering about the weather.

"Isn't it a lovely day today? We were about to take a turn about the park. What do you think, Lu? Oh, let us take a turn about the park."

Lu's eyes met Addy's.

"It would be a pleasure." He bowed vaguely as if he did not know whom to bow to. Then, after a moment's hesitation, he made up his mind and offered an arm to each lady.

Lu's nervousness settled when she took his arm, and they walked under the chestnut trees in the park. She found she enjoyed walking with them, listening to Jessica's chatter and to Addy's responses. Now and then he looked up, and their eyes met. He smiled shyly and looked away.

After half an hour, he took his leave, not without promising to call on them in Grosvenor Square. He lifted his hat and once more smiled shyly at Lu. It warmed her heart.

He really was nice, Lu thought.

"What do you think?" Lu asked Jessica later, after they had returned home.

"He's very nice, Lu. I am positively jealous. But oh," Jessica ran over and gave Lu an unexpectedly fierce hug.

"Oomph."

"You do deserve a man like him. I am so, so, so glad."

Then Jessica burst into tears.

Lu jumped up in alarm. "But Jessica! What on earth is the matter?"

"Nothing." She sobbed into her handkerchief.

Lu pulled her arm around her sister, who leaned against her shoulder, still sobbing.

"It is not easy being a Windmere," she finally said. "I daresay it's a veritable curse."

That, Lu agreed with wholeheartedly.

"They expect me to marry the first man who stands up with me at the ball, but how do I know him, really? He might send flowers, and before you know it, you're shackled for a lifetime." Her nose was red, and tears streamed out of her eyes, but despite all this, she looked more beautiful than ever.

"I agree it is atrocious," said Lu, biding herself to be patient. Surely Jessica would reveal sooner or later what all this had to do with Addy.

"I mean, how does one really know? How does one really choose? There are so many men, it is quite overwhelming."

Lu suppressed a smile. "What a dilemma, indeed."

"Yes, it is. You won't ever know it, and I know it sounds awful, but you are better off as it is. You are lucky to have this one, true friendship. Addy." Her face crumpled. "He's so nice. You have no idea how jealous I am."

Lu decided her nerves were overstrung. She ordered some tea, which Jessica gratefully took. After a cup of tea and having bathed her eyes in cold water, she looked her old self.

"There. Now I feel better. I am so sorry. I've been talking moonshine. Forget what I said. Will you be meeting Addy soon? You should. You will see, you will be married long before I am."

"Jessica! No one's talking about marriage..." Lu's face had flushed scarlet.

Jessica gave her a wise little smile. "Of course not. Forget I said anything at all."

After Jessica dried her face, Lu left for her own room. She fell onto her bed, exhausted.

It had been quite a monumental day.

An odd sort of day.

She couldn't quite decipher what had happened.

Or what she was supposed to be feeling now.

She'd finally met her best friend. Who was everything she ever imagined him to be.

Lu stared at the stuccoed ceiling.

Then why, oh why, was she still so confused?

Chapter Twenty-One

JESSICA WAS RIGHT. THE NEXT DAY, ADDY APPEARED and asked her for a ride in the park.

"Imagine this, he's asked you!" Jessica gushed. "I told you! You will be engaged even before I am!"

Their ride about the park was not long. Most of the time, Lu had no idea what to say. How could this be? How could one have so many things to say in a letter, and nothing at all when one met them in person?

Part of the reason, of course, was that they'd met quite a few acquaintances in the park, and Addy had to stop the curricle every time and greet the people. They'd invariably looked at Lu with astonishment, as if she had no business being seen with Mr Adey, while she squirmed in her seat, wrapped in her shawl.

When they sat once more in silence, Lu decided to pick a topic she knew they both were passionate about: books.

"Have you read *The Imaginary Adulteress?*" she blurted out.

"Goodness, no." He threw her a surprised look. "Who would want to read such drivel?"

"Ah. Uh. Yes. It is drivel. Amusing drivel." Suddenly, Lu felt an inexplicable urge to rave about a book she actually detested. She summarised the story for him in great detail.

Addy shook his head. "I am sorry. It doesn't sound like it's quite the thing for me."

"What about Scott's *Waverley* novels?" Lu asked.

Addy's face brightened. "Oh yes. I found them initially somewhat difficult to get into, but then it engrossed me entirely. What a captivating story!"

"I entirely agree. The only thing I took exception to was that the hero did not marry Flora."

"Did you indeed? I thought he was better off with Rose."

They talked animatedly over this issue, and Lu felt a rush of happiness flush through her as one has when one has an animated conversation with someone who understands what you are talking about.

From there, they moved on to discuss Byron, and a very new, sensational novel by an Anonymous Lady author, *Sense and Sensibility*, which Addy had enjoyed very much; however, Lu very much preferred the said Lady's earlier work named *Pride and Prejudice*. They had engaged in a heated debate when Addy suddenly drew up the curricle with an exclamation of surprise.

Lu hadn't noticed that they were on the South Carriage drive, and the couple who was walking alongside it looked decidedly familiar. As was the maid who trailed after them.

The woman wore a blue coat trimmed with fur, a muff, and her blonde curls bounced as she talked and nodded at her companion, who was none other but St Addington.

"Why, Jessica!" Lu stared at her with surprise. "I had no idea you were here...with St Addington?"

He met her gaze with an ironic lift of the eyebrows and a bow. "Good day to you, Lady Ludmilla. Adam? It is a nice day to be out, is it not?"

Lu snapped her mouth shut.

"Cousin. I had no idea you were out and about with Lady Jessica." Addy looked as astonished as Lu.

"St Addington arrived barely five minutes after you had left with Mr Adey," Jessica chattered. "Aunt allowed us to take a walk since it is such a very fine day, don't you agree?"

Lu registered with a sinking heart that her sister was overexcited. Her eyes were too bright when she looked at St Addington. Could it be? No. It was a preposterous thought. She hadn't fallen in love with him, had she?

"Aunt is here as well. She is talking with Lady Westington over there," Jessica indicated and indeed, there was her aunt, busily talking to a portly lady.

"Shall we continue on, then?" St Addington turned to Jessica with one of his flirtatious smiles, and Jessica blushed and simpered.

Lu felt a jab of jealousy slither in the pit of her stomach.

Now, that was odd.

That did not happen.

Decidedly not.

She turned her head to see St Addington bend over Jessica. It looked like he whispered words of endearment into her ears, for she blushed more and lowered her head.

All the time while her aunt stood by, unaware, chattering to her friend. Aunt! she felt like shouting. St Addington is about to seduce Jessica right under your nose, and you are not noticing.

Lu felt the impulse to jump from the vehicle. She would no doubt twist her ankle, so she gripped the side of the seat to prevent herself from doing precisely that.

She sat, erect, on the curricle with her best friend Addy, and was jealous of the man she'd least expected herself to be jealous of. Addy talked on; he was discussing Mary Wollstonecraft now, but Lu had difficulty focusing on his words.

She felt hot all over; her mind churned, and her stomach made somersaults.

What on earth was happening?

"Would you agree?" Addy turned to her and waited for an answer.

Lu jolted guiltily, for she hadn't heard a single word he said. "I'm sorry. Can you repeat that?"

"Would you agree with Johnson's estimation that, when it comes to comparing Dryden and Pope, with regards to the acquisition of knowledge, Dryden has the more superior mind?"

Lu drew a blank. She stared at Addy, not believing that she could not come up with anything intelligent to say on the matter. This was one of her favourite topics.

"You like Pope. And sugar plums." She hadn't meant to say that. But there it was. "And dogs."

Addy looked aback. "So I do." He smiled. "Not as much as I used to when I was a child, but I do tend to have a definite sweet tooth. And, of course, I like dogs, having one of my own."

"Macbeth."

"Macbeth, indeed. But back to Johnson...."

"I daresay it is easy for a critic to juxtapose two of England's most famous poets and pick their works apart. I daresay both have equal merit. Dryden I enjoy, of course. But Pope is different. It's like comparing apples and pears."

Addy nodded thoughtfully. Then he delved into an analysis of the poetic style of Pope.

Lu sat by him in silence and suppressed a sigh. She wondered why she wasn't at all interested in what he had to say.

Her mind was still with St Addington and Jessica, and she wondered whether she should tell Addy to turn the vehicle around.

After half an hour of expounding upon Johnson's use of language as compared to that of Swift, Lu felt drained and exhausted.

"Thank you for a most intellectually stimulating ride." It had felt more like a literature class than anything else.

And if only they'd not met St Addington and Jessica, she might have actually enjoyed it.

Chapter Twenty-Two

IF APPEARANCES WERE CORRECT, ST ADDINGTON HAD begun to court Jessica. Lu did not like it. She did not like it at all. While eating her eggs at the breakfast table, without really tasting what she was eating, she quietly listened to Jessica gushing on about what plans they had for the day. Regardless of Jessica's protests that St Addington was not the man who'd rescued her from the street, ergo she wasn't in love with him, Lu was convinced that Jessica harboured an infatuation for the man. It troubled her deeply. What troubled her even more was that St Addington seemingly disregarded his own precept of flirting with debutantes. Somehow, it did not apply to Jessica. He was either toying with her, or he was serious about courting her.

Both possibilities worried her.

St Addington was to pick her up for a walk in the afternoon, Jessica explained. Provided Aunt allowed. He'd also talked about taking her to the theatre.

"Theatre? Which one?"

Jessica waved her hand about. "Some little theatre outside town. I forget which. Of course, you and Aunt are meant to come along as well. It is a performance of *The Tempest*. Or something similar. Please, Aunt? May we go?"

"That is all well and good, Jessica, however I must point out that unless St Addington means to court you in earnest, it would be good to remain prudent and keep your cards on the table. Keep a distance from him."

Lu wholeheartedly agreed.

Jessica pulled the corners of her mouth down. "I don't understand, Aunt. At first you insisted that we are seen dancing together, and while he didn't dance with me, he did dance with Lu. And now we are to keep a distance because his reputation is problematic? Why?"

"In the end, St Addington is a good person to have around as a dancing partner. But he isn't good marriage material, despite his wealth and title. I do want you to be happily married, child. There are men other than St Addington with better reputations who have shown a decided interest in you."

"Yes, but I am not interested in any of them. Besides," she said as she buttered the other side of her bread roll, "his cousin Mr Adey is also to come along. And I know for a fact that..." Her voice petered off as she looked at Lu.

Lu buttered her roll with forced concentration.

"Addy? Interesting." There was a decided calculating look in Aunt Ernestina's eyes. "He is a bookish, quiet sort of man, very well behaved and of good stock. If he comes along, of course, that is an entirely different matter. Where is the theatre again?"

Jessica told her.

Aunt Ernestina turned to Lu. "It is decided. We will go to the theatre. And in the afternoon today, you will join them, Lu. It isn't seemly that St Addington takes Jessica out alone to the park. In fact, I may myself go out since the weather is so fine."

Lu cringed. Anything but go along as the third wheel and watch St Addington flirt with Jessica. But how could she say no? She sighed. "Very well, Aunt."

It was every bit as awful as Lu feared it was going to be. Jessica was a chatterbox and talked all the way to the park. St Addington listened with a cynically amused twist on his lips. Now and then, he'd drop a sarcastic comment, which her sister did not understand, and she continued prattling on, which he found even more amusing.

Can't you see he is making fun of you? Lu wanted to scream at her sister. She was also upset at her. Why did she turn into the feather-brained prattle everyone expected her to be whenever he was around? She knew Jessica wasn't really like that.

And why was St Addington flirting with her in that manner?

She glared at him, and his eyes met hers. He lifted his eyebrow inquisitively.

Lu decided she had to take matters into her own hands.

She inserted herself between St Addington and Jessica, taking her arm, and pulled her over to the Serpentine, where a group of children was feeding the ducks.

"Oh! Look! Lady Wilmington is over there. Let us go and say hello." Jessica pulled away from Lu and traipsed ahead, not seeing that St Addington did not follow her.

"Are you joining us at the theatre tonight?" He turned to Lu.

"Yes, for I do enjoy a good play. I believe your cousin is joining us as well?"

"Surprisingly, yes. Normally he doesn't venture very far outside of his comfort zone, which consists of his sofa and his book."

"Indeed? As far as I know, he enjoys the theatre very much." Lu bit down on her bottom lip. She'd almost revealed that she knew so much more about Addy than she should. She ought to be careful when talking to St Addington.

"Hm. You seem to know my cousin rather well in the meantime."

"Maybe. What about you? What intentions do you have towards my sister?" She shot at him.

"Lady Jessica?"

"No. I meant Lady Wilmington." Lu rolled her eyes. "Of course I mean Jessica. I only have her as a sister, don't I?"

"She's pretty enough," he said vaguely.

"That wasn't what I asked." Lu glared at him. "Do you intend to court her?"

He hooded his eyes. "And if I do?"

She narrowed her eyes at him. "My lord. This is my sister. I won't have you toy with her."

"Ah, but Lady Ludmilla. Toying is precisely what I am so good at."

"You may toy all you want, but not with my little sister. I forbid it." She wagged her finger up and down under his nose.

"You forbid it." A flash of irritation crossed his face.

"Yes." She tilted up her chin stubbornly.

"You. *Forbid*. It."

"I. Do."

They stood in front of the Serpentine, glaring at each other. The world shrunk, and she only saw him, the flaring of his nostrils, the curling of his lips, the sudden coldness that entered his eyes.

"You forget who you are talking to. You are taking a great liberty telling me what I can and cannot do, my girl," he said so quietly that she shivered.

Before she could shoot back at him that she was not, and would never be, under any circumstances whatsoever, ever, be "his girl" and how dare he call her that? —a timid voice interrupted them.

"Lu? St Addington?"

Both jerked up their heads.

Jessica stood in front of them, looking from one to another. Behind her stood their aunt, with a perplexed look on her face, and Lady Wilmington, who'd raised her lorgnette at them.

For how long had they stood there, watching them fight?

St Addington cursed under his breath, only for Lu

171

and Jessica to hear. Jessica gasped. Lu rolled her eyes. Then suddenly, a charming smile spread over his face. "You see, we have been squabbling, Lady Ludmilla and I, over who is the better actor. Kean or Garrick. Lady Ludmilla is of the firm conviction that it is Garrick. Which, as an admirer of Kean, I cannot possibly accept."

The man lies so glibly, Lu thought with admiration. What would she give to be able to do the same!

He took off his hat, and with a flick of his head flung his locks back before he placed the hat on his head again.

Then he kissed the hands of all three ladies with an elegant bow, and bid them farewell until tonight, where they surely would be able to see he was right, and she was incontrovertibly wrong when they saw Kean on stage.

He also lifted Lu's hand and kissed it, with a wink.

Then he was gone.

Lu looked after him, blinking.

"What has that been about?" Jessica demanded, voicing her thoughts.

Her aunt drew her aside. "You must be careful, Ludmilla."

Lu sighed. "I know. I know. He is a dangerous flirt."

Her aunt looked at her, an odd expression on her face. "I actually did not see him flirt with you at all. Which is what rather worries me."

Her aunt's words haunted Lu the remainder of the day.

OF ALL THE SOCIAL FUNCTIONS, Lu was more amenable towards going to the theatre, even though here,

172

too, she had qualms. At least one could sit in the back and remain unobserved while she observed others.

When Adam Adey came in the evening to pick them up, Lu was glad to see him.

Addy was reliable, she told herself. He was her good, old friend, with whom one knew what to expect. She could chat books with him; there would be no double-entendre, no indecent teasing, no exhausting arguing with the man.

Addy was safe.

She was glad they were friends.

It did not hurt that he looked handsome in his black tailcoat and breeches, with a crispy white shirt that ruffed under his chin. Not quite as handsome as his dashing cousin, of course, but close enough. Besides, St Addington was a category of his own.

They went in the coach together to the theatre; however, without St Addington.

"I don't understand why St Addington would insist on inviting us to the theatre and then not appear himself," Aunt Ernestina complained. She was wearing a massive turban with purple plumes that brushed against the ceiling of the carriage.

"I am certain he will appear," Adam said soothingly. "He has a tendency to be late." He helped Jessica out of the carriage, and she beamed at him.

"Ah, here he is." St Addington appeared seemingly out of nowhere, dressed to perfection in black tailcoat and breeches, crisp white shirt points and silver waist-coat. Lu swallowed. Once more, she felt like shrinking against the wall when she beheld the glamour and the splendour of the place.

St Addington nodded at her curtly and was in an unusually restless mood. After he'd assigned each person a seat in his box, he excused himself again and left.

"Well. That is decidedly odd," Jessica noted with a frown.

Lu thought so, too. She was disappointed that the seat next to her was empty. Never mind, she was determined to enjoy this play. It was rare for her to have the opportunity to go to the theatre.

The first Act began, and St Addington still did not join them. After a while, she forgot about him as she immersed herself in the play.

Kean truly was fantastic. As was the entire ensemble. The props were elaborate and beautifully made.

Then Caliban arrived. Hunchbacked, he stomped onto the stage, his long coat draping on the ground, his long hair hung into his face.

What an interesting figure! Lu would've loved to show him to Addy. How Addy would love this—oh. Addy was sitting right there, next to Jessica, bending over her, pointing out that Caliban's beard was no doubt artificial.

Lu turned back to the stage, and something struck her as odd.

What was odd was that Caliban somehow seemed familiar to her, except she could not, for the life of her, pinpoint what it was.

She'd never seen the figure played so well before. His voice was loud, deep and hoarse, his movements daring;

the audience was riveted. It was a movement of the head as he flung his hair back.

Lu gasped. She clenched her fingers into the velvet upholstery of her chair.

It was impossible. It couldn't be!

But there he was, so very clearly, on stage in disguise for all to see.

The Viscount St Addington was Caliban.

"How DISOBLIGING of St Addington to disappear thus," her aunt complained during recess. "I am very cross with the man. Addy, you must convey our displeasure to him when you see him later."

"I do apologise for my cousin. It is badly mannered of him, indeed." Lu watched Addy closely. But his demeanour was unruffled and did not reveal that he knew his cousin had just been on stage.

"Though I must say," her aunt continued, "the play was very well done. Especially Caliban. Who is the actor again?"

"Richard Ridley." Addy ushered them out of the box into the refreshment room, which was crammed with people.

"Never heard of the fellow." Her aunt lifted her lorgnette to study the crush of people in front of them.

"He's relatively new. Very talented, I'd say." Lu looked at him closely. His face was calm. "He looked somewhat familiar," she mused. "Wouldn't you agree?"

Addy turned to her, amused. "The fellow was one of

175

the most hideous creatures on stage. Who do you think he resembles, poor man?"

Lu decided to be straightforward. "There was something about his mannerism that reminded me somewhat of your cousin."

Addy coughed.

"St Addington!" That was Jessica, who'd taken Addy's other arm. "I do disagree, Lu. Caliban has a hideous nose, almost like a potato, and a tremendous hunchback. But St Addington is quite beautiful. I know you dislike St Addington, but how monstrous of you to compare the two."

"You're right. I must be blind. Forget it." Lu waved it away.

Addy, however, gave her a piercing look. When she met his gaze, he turned his lips into a quick smile. Then his eyes slid away.

Aunt Ernestine fanned herself with the peacock fan. "Can one have some champagne, you think? It is dreadfully stuffy in here, and I am quite thirsty."

"Your servant, ma'am." Addy boxed himself through the crowd and returned with a footman who brought the desired champagne.

Lu gratefully took a glass and sipped from it.

Her aunt discussed the newest gossip with Lady Adkins, who sat in the box next to theirs, as Addy listened with a smile to Jessica discussing the play.

Lu leaned against the marble bust and fanned herself. It was rather warm in the room, and all the excitement made her even hotter.

"You're not actually going to marry her, are you?"

She heard a male voice drawl from the other side of the statue.

"Of course not. I doubt we will make it even half-way to Gretna." A snicker.

The hair on Lu's arm stood on end.

She knew that voice. That nasal voice. That snicker.

She'd heard it before. That day in the library. She was hiding with St Addington behind the curtain while a man proposed to the lady to elope with him to Gretna Green.

"Your aim, Stilton, is what precisely?"

A sniff and a snort of someone taking a pinch of snuff.

"Revenge, naturally."

"By ruining the daughter. I say, I like your style."

"Both her father and her brother wouldn't deign to lower themselves to even greet my lowly self. When I tried it the honourable way, marched into the house to propose, they kicked me down the stairs. I am too lowly for his daughter."

"Typical for Macclesfield. He is mighty high in the instep."

"Duke or not, I won't have it. He will look neither particularly intelligent nor high in the instep the moment he notices his daughter's ruined, and no one will have her no more. I'll be good enough for him then, mark my words."

"Prime plan, Stilton."

The voices came closer. Lu pressed herself against the wall and hoped the statue hid her sufficiently.

The men stood right next to her. She could smell the

floral perfume of Lord Eustachius Stilton, mixed with sweat. She nearly gagged.

They passed by her. Lu glanced up, and recognised the dandy in purple waistcoat, who was Stilton, and the other gentleman with the drawly voice, whom she recognised as Lord Hargreaves. Her aunt was fleetingly acquainted with him.

Neither gentleman had seen Lu.

Her heart hammered and her palms were sweaty.

It was like she felt a replay of the scene she'd found herself in, so long ago.

She clenched her hands into fists.

Macclesfield's daughter. She was a pretty, vapid thing. Lu was not closely acquainted with her, for she was one of the ladies who never really saw Lu. Lu had assumed that the love between them was mutual, but it appeared it was not so. She felt sorry for the girl.

Lu returned to her seat with her mind whirling.

"Ah, there you are, Lady Ludmilla. We worried that after having lost St Addington, we'd also lost you. But here you are, and everything is well." Addy helped her to her seat.

"There were so many people everywhere, it is rather easy to get lost," Lu's voice was breathless.

Throughout the remaining play, Lu had difficulty concentrating. Her mind was with the scene she'd just overheard. Then, Caliban trotted on stage again, and she forgot Macclesfield's daughter and focused entirely on him.

Was he, or was he not, St Addington? Maybe she had merely imagined it? But then again, that movement. It was so like him. Was it a coincidence? Where was he, if not on stage right now? Could it be possible that St Addington led a double life as an actor? Somehow, it wouldn't surprise her. It would be exactly the kind of thing St Addington would do.

How much, she wondered, of him was sincere, and how much an act? Was that what he was doing most of the time, putting up an act, the act of the rake?

There had been some rare glimpses of the man where she thought she'd seen him for who he was.

I really don't understand him at all, Lu concluded.

Chapter Twenty-Three

HE FELT EVERY FIBRE OF HIS BEING SIZZLE WITH LIFE when he stood on stage. Tonight had been one of his best performances, ever. When he was on stage, when he climbed into a role, he became that character. He forgot everything around him. He forgot himself, who he acted for, and he disappeared into a world that was entirely make believe. It was wonderful.

No one had ever suspected who he really was. No one knew his real identity. More than once, he'd looked up at the balcony on the left, and he'd seen her sitting there.

For some reason, he didn't know why, he'd been particularly energised knowing she was there.

He'd been acting for her.

Then, the applause. He'd seen her get up and applaud.

A rush of giddy happiness rushed through his veins.

This was life.

This.

"I AM to tell you that Lady Rutherford is very cross with you," Adam told him later that evening, when they were both at home.

"Is she? I suppose she would be." St Addington attempted to twirl his hat on the tip of his stick. He'd had too much to drink, in celebration of a performance well done. Kean himself had clapped him on the shoulder and congratulated him. His breast swelled with pride every time he thought of it.

"Be careful. Lady Ludmilla almost recognised you."

The hat he'd been attempting to twirl dropped to the ground. "She did? Of course, she would. Clever girl," he muttered almost to himself. "What did she say? Did she like the play? Did she like—me?"

"Yes, she liked it. Of course she did. She thought that there were some similarities between Caliban and you. In terms of mannerism."

"The devil. She might have said that just to be provocative. We had a bit of a quarrel earlier, so it might not mean at all that she has recognised me. She may have tried to shred my character because of our quarrel."

"I am not sure. She is very sharp-eyed."

"Sharp-eyed and sharp-tongued. She also has a sharp mind." St Addington strolled over to the table to pour himself a glass of brandy. He lifted the decanter and looked inquisitively at Adam.

"No thank you." Adam sat down and crossed his legs.

"You like her, don't you?" St Addington took a sip from his glass.

"Lady Ludmilla?"

"Hm."

"Of course I do." Adam flushed.

"You have been corresponding with her."

Adam threw him a surprised look.

St Addington waved his glass about. "Richards may have mentioned once or twice that there are letters from Rutherford house, and they were not for me."

"Er. Yes. We have corresponded. A little." Adam's flush deepened. "Mainly about books. It has abated lately, however."

St Addington noted the flush and nodded into his glass thoughtfully.

Adam looked troubled. "I need to ask you something, Cousin."

"I am all ears."

Adam took a big breath. "When you told me the other day that you were considering marriage, I assumed you were not funning."

St Addington stared into the brown liquid of his glass as he twirled it about. "Hm. I might have not."

"My question is as follows: if you are serious about marriage, why are you not courting the girl?"

St Addington blinked. "But I am. Went out for a walk in the park yesterday. Sent her flowers. Went to the park today as well. Sent flowers." He ticked it off his fingers. "Will be going to the park again tomorrow. Will make sure to send more flowers, dash it. What more ought a fellow be doing?"

Adam blinked. "You are asking me that?"

St Addington shrugged. "Took her to the theatre tonight. Fine, I wasn't exactly in her company. But we were in the same room." He grinned.

"Oh, Adrian, do be serious." Adam rubbed his eyebrow.

"Oh, but I am. I don't think I've ever been as serious about a woman." St Addington stared into his glass.

"Yes but—forgive me if I say this—but you yourself indicated earlier at one point that Lady Ludmilla does not yet seem to return your regard. You may be right that she may have taken you into dislike for some reason or other. If she did, you have only yourself to blame."

St Addington looked up, startled. "Lady Ludmilla? Are we talking about Lady Ludmilla?"

Now Adam looked startled. "Why, yes?" He shook his head. "Which of the two Windmere girls were you talking about?"

St Addington gave him a piercing stare. "Whichever one you are thinking of, it's the other one."

Adam stared back. "The other one. How am I supposed to make sense of that? You are speaking in riddles. You are also flirting heavily with both, scoundrel that you are."

St Addington uttered a short laugh. "Are we talking at cross purposes? I have been trying rather hard to court Lady Jessica, of course."

A pause.

"Lady Jessica." Adam got up and poured himself a glass of brandy. "I see."

"She is a diamond of the first water."

"So she is."

"Not quite as sharp-tongued as her sister," St Addington mused. "Nor as sharp-minded."

"I wouldn't say that, precisely. Lady Jessica is not a

bluestocking like her sister, but she has a fine mind." Adam got up. "If you will excuse me, Cousin, I'm rather tired. I will retire to my room."

St Addington waved him away.

After Adam had left, he stared into his brandy glass. "Interesting," he muttered, then downed the remains of his brandy. "Very interesting."

Chapter Twenty-Four

THE NEXT DAY, FLOWERS ARRIVED FOR BOTH Ludmilla and Jessica.

"Roses," Jessica said, "Red roses." She buried her head in a bouquet to hide her blush.

"St Addington," Aunt Ernestine said with a disapproving sniff, reading his card. "It appears he may be serious, after all. How excessively odd."

"Why odd, Aunt? A gentleman who woos me and you find it odd?" Jessica pouted. "He's not only a gentleman but a lord, too. A good catch. If one forgets about his reputation, that is."

Aunt merely sniffed and did not reply.

Lu had received her bouquet with a smile. It was a colourful, cheerful bouquet consisting of tulips, carnations, and peonies. The card that came with it was signed by Adam Adey. *Addy always knows what I like best,* Lu thought fondly. Suddenly it hit her that if Addy were ever to propose, she would accept. She could imagine nothing better than setting up house with Addy. Her cottage, with the chickens, and Addy sitting on the bench in front of the house, reading a book and discussing Pope. The sky was blue, and the sun shone. It was a comfortable, cosy picture.

And a tad bit boring.

But well. Better boring than disloyal, unfaithful, and rakish.

Like Matthew.

Like St Addington.

ONE AFTERNOON, they were invited to Lady Somerset's winter picnic, to which Aunt Ernestine insisted they go. Lu had never been to a winter picnic.

"It's the newest thing. Instead of summer drinks, they serve mulled wine and gingerbread biscuits," Jessica explained. "Though I daresay I will be too cold to sit on a blanket on the frozen floor. I hope they will have a fire where we can warm ourselves."

"Make sure to dress warmly and bring your furs and muffs," Ernestina intervened. "And, if you happen to meet St Addington, Jessica, which is likely, you will thank him prettily for the roses, and then proceed to take a walk with Lord Horton. He is an earl and has shown a marked interest in you lately."

Jessica folded her hands in her lap and looked down. "Very well, Aunt."

Lu threw Jessica a surprised look. Why was her sister so unexpectedly docile?

"And you, Ludmilla, will of course accept Adam Adey when he asks for a walk."

"Of course."

Lu did not mind that in the least. They would discuss books as they walked, and that suited her very well.

As with so many things in life, things came about differently. Lord Horton, who had every intention of walking with Jessica, was dragged away by a very determined Philippa Peddleton. Adam ended up running after Jessica's scarf, for a sudden gust of wind had blown it towards the lake, with Jessica scurrying after him, so that Lu found herself staring, once more, into the sardonic gaze of St Addington, who mutely held out his arm. They walked along a small forest path that led to a pagoda in a clearing. It was hidden behind the trees, and the voices of the other people fell away. In summertime the place must be wonderful, it occurred to Lu. But now, the trees were bare, and the ground was barren brown. Lu found she liked the stark landscape.

"Leave it to Lady Somerset to arrange a winter picnic, of all things," St Addington said. "Yet we have neither ice nor snow to entertain ourselves with."

"I rather like it. It's different. It is better to be out here in the fresh, cool air than in the stuffy ballrooms."

"Like the theatre."

"Like the theatre." Their eyes met.

"I heard you enjoyed the play the other night. I was, unfortunately, detained and unable to join you after all." He fiddled around with the cuff of his coat.

"Ah, yes. You missed a wonderful performance. It was a most interesting experience."

He brightened. "Did you think so, indeed? What, pray, did you enjoy most about the play?"

"Kean, of course. He is a master at acting."

"Of course. Of course. Kean is spectacular, I have always said so." He looked at her with expectation. "Anything or anyone else you enjoyed?"

Lu bit down a smile. "Most of the actors were very talented."

"Most?"

"Well yes. Most."

"Who, er, would you consider to be included in 'most'?"

Lu pretended to study the slanted roof of the pagoda. "I liked Miranda and Ariel, of course."

"And?" He looked at her expectantly.

"And?"

"What about Caliban?"

"The acting in general was very well done. Arresting, amusing, even."

"He gave an excellent performance, did he not? I mean, not that I would know about it, since I wasn't there. But I heard that he was good."

Lu stared at him, deadpan. "It was you, wasn't it?"

"Me?" He faced her with surprise.

She turned on him. "You are an actor, are you not? You played Caliban. No need to pretend otherwise. I recognised you. The hunchback looked awfully, painfully real. How did they do it?"

"Pillows. And?"

"And what?"

"Did you like it?" There was expectation on his face as if her answer mattered to him.

She hesitated.

"Well?"

"It was brilliant. You were brilliant."

He exhaled. "Do you really think so?"

"Of course. You embody Caliban perfectly. Of course, I have not seen too many renditions of *The Tempest* to compare, but it was very well done. You are a talented actor. So this is what you do, in secret?"

"What made you realise it was me?"

"I am not certain. A movement by the hand, by the head, the way you fling your head back sometimes, something you tend to do," Lu thought, and shook her head. "In the end, I am not sure what it was, exactly, that gave you away."

St Addington grinned at her like a schoolboy. "Very perceptive of you, Lady Lu."

"I can't imagine that no one else has recognised you."

"People are not normally as perceptive as one would think they could be. They hear and see all sorts of things without ever guessing the truth."

"How long have you been acting?"

"For several years. I am learning with Kean himself." They walked up the steps to the pagoda. It wasn't very big, but a wooden structure with four pillars and a bench in the middle.

"Who would have thought the Viscount St Addington leads a double life," Lu said teasingly as she sat down on the bench. "But never fear, your secret is safe with me."

"We all have secrets, do we not?" There was something in his eyes that she couldn't quite identify.

She looked away quickly. "Speaking of secrets. At the

theatre, I overheard two gentlemen discuss Cynthia Vanheal."

He leaned against a wooden pillar and crossed his arms and booted legs. "Vanheal?"

"You know. The Duke of Macclesfield's daughter. The lady in the library with the dainty feet? When we were hiding behind the curtain? You were right that it was Lord Stilton. He told the other gentleman, whom I believe to be Lord Hargreaves, that he was not really eloping with Miss Vanheal. His intention is to ruin her. To revenge himself on her father. Who happens to be the Duke of Macclesfield."

"Sounds rather melodramatic."

Lu jumped up. "That is all you have to say? That it is melodramatic?"

He shrugged. "What else should I say? One of my precepts is to never meddle in another man's affairs, especially if they involve women."

"A lady's reputation is at stake here."

"And?"

Lu stomped her foot. Unfortunately, it did not make any impact at all.

"How typical of you! I don't know why I expected anything else of you. When you have already proven yourself to be of a most callous nature, especially when it comes to ladies' reputations."

"Oho! It appears the Lady Ludmilla does listen to gossip about the rakely deeds of St Addington after all."

"This isn't gossip. I have personally seen you at your worst."

His face turned to stone. "Pray elaborate, Lady Ludmilla. When, or what exactly are we talking about?"

"At the Whittlesborough ball. Ten years ago." She took a big breath. "When Matthew Fredericks was still one of your cronies."

Her words hung in the air.

"So you do remember, Lady Ludmilla. I'd begun to wonder whether you would," he said softly.

She turned her head to him jerkily. "Of course I remember. I remember every single dastardly word that was spoken in that card room."

"I confess I can barely remember the incident myself. I daresay I was rather foxed. Pray remind me what exactly was spoken?" He'd transformed, from one moment to the next, from the relaxed, charming gentleman to the sneering rake of the card room.

She struggled with herself. Then she decided it did not matter anymore. She tilted up her chin. "You said to Matthew Fredericks, I quote, '*I bet you a hundred guineas even you can't work up the courage to kiss the homeliest Windmere woman with your eyes open.*'"

St Addington stared. Then he threw his head back and—laughed.

"How dare you. How dare you laugh about this." Lu's lips had turned white.

"Forgive me. I must have been more foxed than I thought. What an inane thing to say. Throw a group of drunken hard-core gamblers together, and what do you think will happen? You did not truly expect us to discuss Dryden and Pope? If it is any solace, we also bet on all sorts of other naughty things, which I dare not elaborate for they are not for a lady's ears."

"Oh! Now you're saying, 'it's how we men are' and 'this is how we speak,' and that somehow makes it all right? I think it's profoundly despicable behaviour."

"What's that saying again? An eavesdropper never hears any good of herself?" He leaned against the column with a smug smile playing about his lips.

A rush of fury shot through Lu. How dare he downplay the incident and shift the blame on her, as if she deserved what she'd heard? "I did not eavesdrop on purpose. In fact, I was standing right there, and no one saw me. It is vile of you to claim otherwise."

He rubbed his forehead. "You are right."

"And I—what did you say?"

"I said you're right. I owe you an apology." He bowed prettily.

She gaped at him. How dare he apologise so unexpectedly and pull the rug from under her?

"It must have hurt you badly enough for you to remember the exact words all these years. Ten years. Good heavens. And you recall every word. They were never meant for you to hear, and you are entirely right, it is a vile thing to have said to begin with." He shook his head. "I have no excuse other than that I was rather foxed."

"I. Well." Lu did not know what to reply.

"And Matthew? He took me by my word?"

"I don't know." She blinked hard.

"Interesting." He looked at her speculatively. "So, he never did try to kiss you?"

Lu crossed her arms. "I seem to recall that he replied that he only wanted to marry me for my fortune. I broke off contact afterwards."

"Did you, now? Consequently, I may have actually done you a service, eh?"

There was some truth to what he said, but Lu would admit this only over her dead body. Since he was so conveniently standing in front of her, he had to bear the entire brunt of the blame.

"You also said that you would triple the wager."

"What an excellent memory you have," he said softly, and stepped towards her.

She took a step back, and the back of her legs hit the wooden balustrade. He took another step forward. She had nowhere to go. He stemmed both his arms alongside her against the pillar, pinning her down.

"What a fool I was," he murmured. The hair on her arms stood on end.

"I dare you." Lu thought she must be stark raving mad, even as she heard the words herself. "I dare you to kiss the homeliest Windmere woman with your eyes open." She tilted up her chin defiantly.

His gaze dropped from her eyes to her lips. "Dare accepted."

Lu held her breath. He bent his head. Her heart fluttered wildly, and her stomach somersaulted. His mouth covered hers hungrily, his firm mouth demanding a response. Her entire body tingled from head to toe.

She did the unthinkable and kissed him back. Then, she opened her eyes, for she had involuntarily closed them.

She drowned in a sea of blue-green.

This, she thought.

This.

She wanted the kiss to go on forever. Somehow, one hand had crawled up and dug into his locks, and her other hand clung to his shoulder, and his mouth began to trail away from her lips along her jaw to her ears, in a string of delicious butterfly kisses.

Then he suddenly froze, lifted his head, and hissed a loud and long curse.

"Wha—what?" Lu dropped her hand and turned around.

Outside on the path leading to the pagoda stood a couple.

Philippa Peddleton and Lord Horton stared at them, shocked.

Chapter Twenty-Five

It was quite a feat, the *TON* gossiped, that Lady Ludmilla Windmere, daughter of a duke and epitome of propriety and good conduct, had managed to thoroughly ruin herself. Miss Penelope Peddleton and Lord Horton had done an assiduous job in spreading this delicious piece of latest gossip. It spread faster, wider, and with more glutinous determination than the fog that seeped over the River Thames in the early morning.

She was a spinster! A plain old maid. An ape leader! Kissing London's most beloved and notorious rake! Publicly in the park, for everyone to see. How dare she? Spinsters did not kiss. Especially not rakes. Ever.

What was this world coming to that even the spinsters were falling under St Addington's spell?

Oh, but it was not surprising, other voices said cruelly. It was St Addington after all. He would seduce a monkey if he could. Could one really expect differently of St Addington?

Thus gossip went. Followed by tittering, gasps of fake horror and more gossip.

Ludmilla, who normally did not hold much with gossip, had no defence, for alas, this time the rumours were entirely, sadly, incontrovertibly true. What was worse: it was her own fault. For she'd veritably goaded St Addington into kissing her. And she'd kissed him back.

The best—or the worst—of it was that she did not regret it. Not one whit.

"Bring me that tonic." Aunt Ernestine was lying on the sofa, in Aunt Mildred's manner, her hand over her eyes, as if the daylight pained her.

Things must be bad indeed if they'd brought down Aunt Ernestine. Lu nestled at the pommel of her reticule, feeling like a school child in disgrace, which, of course, she was.

The maid brought the hartshorn salt.

"Not this." Aunt Ernestine waved it away. "I want that other stuff. Dr Rothely's Purging Elixir. Purging all the horror and shock of the last hour out of my body is exactly what I need at the moment. What on earth were you thinking, child?" She wrung her hands.

"What's it like?" Jessica had drawn Lu into the other corner of the drawing room. She lowered her voice. "Kissing a rake, I mean."

Lu thought. She could come up with an entire range of words. Surprising. Exhilarating. Passionate. If she had to choose only one ... "Magical."

Jessica clasped her hands together. "Oh, was it, really? How exciting!"

Aunt Ernestine, who heard like a hawk, said, "Exciting, poppycock. You will have to marry him now."

"No."

Aunt Ernestine sat up. "My hearing must be failing. Did you just say 'no'?"

"But Lu, all of London is talking. Your reputation is gone. No one will admit you now. No one. I daresay my marriage prospects are gone as well. I agree with aunt that the best thing to do is to just marry him." Jessica beamed.

"I don't know why you appear to be so inordinately happy about me having ruined my reputation and your marriage prospects being gone," Lu grumbled.

"I am not happy," Jessica retorted with an enormous grin on her face. "I am merely being practical. And maybe you are right, I am indeed happy that you get to marry before me. I always said you would, didn't I?"

Lu groaned.

"At least one of the girls seems to be in possession of some common sense." Ernestine poured half of the elixir into a glass of water and drank it all up in one gulp. "Ludmilla. My dear, dear girl! When I said that a Windmere woman is a married woman, I did not mean that you should throw away your reputation in panic to achieve this aim, least of all to St Addington, of all men. Mind you, he is a good catch, he has a title, and his fortune is also not to be despised. But why must you choose a rake and a scallywag, of all the eligible men that are out there?"

"I certainly did not scheme any of this, Aunt," Lu

replied, stung. "You must believe me that I am, in fact, rather determined to remain unwed."

"There is no way out of it now. You will marry him, and that is final."

Lu opened her mouth to protest when the butler appeared. "A gentleman is here to see you, ma'am."

Lu tensed up immediately.

He lifted the calling card. "A Mr Adam Adey."

Lu exhaled audibly in relief.

"Accompanied by the Viscount St Addington."

Lu inhaled sharply.

"The scoundrel!" Aunt Ernestine scrambled up and patted her hair. "Send them in, immediately. And oh, James, also tea."

"Yes, my lady."

Tea? How could they all sit in the drawing room as if she hadn't just shared the most earth-shattering kiss with St Addington and drink tea? What to do? What to do? She could hear the male voices in the foyer. Rushing out of the door was out of the question.

Lu's gaze flew hectically to the window. Could she—? They were two storeys up from the ground. She could fling the window open and—But of course, not. She was being ridiculous.

She walked woodenly to a chair and sat down. Jessica sat next to her and pressed her cold hands in reassurance.

The gentlemen entered the room. Lu jumped up again and curtsied, before dropping into her chair again.

Awkward silence settled over the room as James brought in a tea pot and a dish full of comfits. He arranged everything on the table, then left.

St Addington had this quizzical, slightly sardonic look on his face that he wore whenever he felt defensive.

Addy's forehead was folded to a worried frown. "You must forgive this intrusion. But I—that is, we—have concluded that the best thing is to discuss this matter calmly and reasonably like the adults that we are. There is no question that St Addington here, of course, will do the right thing."

"Will I." He folded his arms and studied the plate of sweets in front of him with intent interest.

"St Addington." Aunt Ernestine pulled herself up to haughty heights. "What are you implying?"

"He isn't implying anything," Addy intervened hastily. "The scandal is undoubtedly momentous, and I can't for the life of me imagine what went through his brains—or lack thereof—jeopardising Lady Ludmilla's reputation, for contrary to common talk, I know my cousin to be quite a different person entirely, but what is done is done and can't be helped. Everything will be rectified, and all will be well in the end. You will see."

St Addington pinched the bridge of his nose. "Adam. Be quiet. Here, have a sugar plum." He held the silver plate under Addy's nose. Addy waved it away.

"You, my lord," Aunt Ernestine said awfully, wagging her finger at him, "have gone one step too far. You have ruined the reputation of a Windmere woman. No one, I repeat, no one does this without impunity."

St Addington shrank in his chair.

It seemed to Lu that he appeared to be uncommonly nervous. With Aunt Ernestine bullying him and wagging her finger at him, he had every reason to be. But it appeared to Lu that it was more than that. When their eyes met briefly, when he'd entered the room just now, there'd been something unspoken in them. A question. It had thrown Lu in confusion. But then he looked away, and she thought she'd merely imagined it.

It was evident he didn't want to marry her. She did not deceive herself for one moment that his presence now meant anything to the contrary. He was a rake, and rakes in general did not want to marry. He was no different in that regard.

Well, neither did she.

She did not want to be married to someone who did not want her.

Maybe he'd never even wanted to kiss her in the first place. She'd goaded him, challenged him into kissing her. Since he was a rake, he naturally could not resist.

How terrible that maybe he would never have kissed her out of his own will if she hadn't challenged him to! The notion rankled.

Now everyone seemed to ask her what she wanted. How could she say that when she did not know herself?

She wanted...oh, she did not know what she wanted.

Once upon a time, she wanted to be married to Addy.

Addy, her best friend. Addy, who knew her as no one else in this world did. The Addy of the letters, not the gentleman who sat across from her in flesh and blood. He was nice enough, and she did like him.

He defended her, specks of red flecked his cheeks, as though he took this matter very personally.

A rush of affection flushed through her.

202

Yes, Addy was important to her. They were good friends.

But she wanted more.

She wanted love. Was that too much to ask?

Suddenly, all the eyes were on Lu. What had they been saying? She had been wool gathering and not paying any attention to their chatter.

"I suppose a speechless stare is a response as well. I will take that as a negative." St Addington popped a sugar plum into his mouth.

"Ludmilla." Her aunt wrung her hands. "The Viscount has just asked you whether you want to marry him."

"Oh."

Finally, a proposal of marriage, and she'd completely missed the moment.

St Addington's shoulders were shaking with quiet laughter.

Lu glared at him. He was evidently enjoying every moment of her suffering, the scoundrel. "But don't you see? He doesn't really want to marry me! And I don't want you to bully him into proposing to me."

"My dear girl, it seems to be commonly agreed upon in this room that what I want or don't want appears to be beside the point. As far as I am concerned, the issue is what *you* want." Again that look in his eyes. What on earth did it mean?

Lu jumped up and wrung her hands.

"I don't know what I want!" Lu wailed. "Would you all just stop staring at me and leave me in peace!"

"Do you want us to leave you alone with the

viscount, dear?" her aunt said with an uncustomary gentle voice.

Heaven forbid. "No! I'm sorry. It's just a bit too much right now. I do know one thing." She took a big breath. "I do not want to marry you, St Addington. I don't want us to be married to one another and grow to hate each other because of a silly k—kiss."

"Well. There it is." St Addington threw up his hands in an ironic gesture, but his eyes were icy.

"You are entirely in the right when you say that what you want or do not want is beside the point," Aunt Ernestine put in with a voice of steel. "Because it does not matter one bit what either of you want. Your reputation is in tatters, Ludmilla." She pointed her finger at St Addington. "And you will marry her."

"Not happening if the lady refuses." St Addington shrugged. "Your intentions in all honour, ma'am, but I have my principles, too. I do not force ladies. Ever. And this lady has made her sentiment more than clear."

"Adrian!" Addy jumped up and took an agitated turn about the room. He stopped in front of Lu, visibly struggling with himself. "I cannot bear this. If you will not marry to save Lady Ludmilla from certain ruin, then I will."

Jessica gasped.

Addy went down on his knees in front of Lu. "Lady Ludmilla. Will you do me the honour of accepting my name and my hand in marriage?"

"How heroic of you," St Addington noted. "And very prettily done. Must take a leaf out of your book next time."

"Be quiet, Adrian," Addy, gentle Addy, snarled. "Lady Ludmilla?"

Lu stared down at her Addy. His blond hair was finer than St Addington's lion mane, and showed the beginning of a slightly receding hairline, but his grey eyes were full of solicitous concern.

He was sincere.

"My dear friend," Lu's voice wobbled slightly. "I am so grateful. Indeed, all these years I have been proud to be able to call you my friend. You must believe me that there is no greater honour to receive a proposal of marriage from you. With all my heart. I feel so honoured. But," her eyes teared up, "you must believe me that I cannot accept your sacrifice, even if it is done out of friendship and loyalty."

A look of bemusement crossed Addy's face.

"Sounds like she won't have you, either," St Addington translated cheerfully. "Too bad, old chap. Better luck next time."

Aunt Ernestina groaned. "She just turned down two perfectly acceptable marriage proposals. This girl will bring me to my early grave. Where is the elixir? And why are you crying, Jessica? This is a madhouse. A madhouse, I say!"

Everything indeed seemed to have erupted into chaos. Everyone was talking at the same time except for Jessica, who was sobbing noisily into her handkerchief.

Addy and St Addington were arguing.

Lu knelt on the floor, attempting to talk to Jessica.

Then the butler burst in, asking whether they wanted another pot of tea.

Aunt Ernestine eventually ceased her monologue of lament and snapped at the poor butler, as if everything were his fault.

When the men took their leave, St Addington shot Lu a penetrating glance, took his top hat and pulled a protesting Addy out of the room.

Her aunt retired, complaining that her head was pounding most ferociously, and would somebody go out and buy more of that elixir? Jessica had run up to her room, still crying.

Only Lu remained in the drawing room. She sat down with a sigh and poured herself some fresh tea. It was too good to let spoil.

Then her eyes fell on the silver plate with sweets.

She stared at it.

Her hand shook as it crept to cover her mouth in dawning realisation.

St Addington had picked off all the sugar plums from the plate and eaten them.

Only the sugar plums.

Every single one of them.

Chapter Twenty-Six

Lu WAS RUNNING AWAY.

From her aunt and Jessica, from gossip and scandal. From her own confused thoughts and feelings.

Yes, it was cowardly.

Yes, Aunt Ernestine and Jessica had protested violently and done their best to convince her to stay.

Yes, she probably ought to have had a final conversation with either of the Addys (confound it!) to clear up the matter.

But she simply could not bear to stay in London a moment longer. She'd packed her trunks the very next day and left.

She was a pariah now, her reputation ruined, in tatters, gone.

Oddly enough, that did not matter half as much to her than the fact that she'd gotten everything wrong about Addy.

Addy, whom she'd thought was St Addington, then Adam Adey, then St Addington again. Her first instinct had been correct, until she'd been led astray by St Addington himself, then his cousin, who happened to have the same nickname. Why did St Addington never clear up the confusion to begin with, when they were already corresponding? Why had he allowed her to call him by his cousin's nickname? Surely, St Addington must have known at that dinner party that this would've confused Lu? Yet he'd allowed it to happen. He'd never, not once, attempted to righten the misunderstanding.

He'd been playing a cat and mouse game, simply because he found it amusing. He'd purposely led her astray, even inveigling his own cousin in the charade. Had St Addington talked Adam into posing as Addy? She had to admit to herself that she wasn't certain, for Adam had always seemed authentic.

On the other hand...when she weighed every word she'd exchanged with Adam, he'd never actually talked about their letters...had he?

The mistake may have honestly been on her side, but she also could not discount St Addington having been up to mischief.

Why had this gone so horribly wrong?

Why had St Addington so purposefully deceived her?

She felt sick in her stomach. Lu leaned her hot forehead against the cold window, and it bumped against the glass as the coach rattled along the country road to Bath.

She could analyse this to the death of it, fact was that no matter how she twisted and turned the matter, Addy—her Addy—simply wasn't who she thought he was, never had been, never would be. He'd only ever existed in her imagination.

It was a confounded situation.

She'd never thought she'd be glad to return to Great Aunt Mildred's tomb of a house. Lying in a dark room with curtains closed for the remainder of the year was exactly what she needed.

The clattering of the hooves ceased, and the coach came to a standstill.

Lu awoke from her trance, opened the carriage door.

"The horse has lost a horseshoe," the coachman grumbled. "Might as well take a turn about while I fix it."

Lu got off the coach and looked about.

She took in the gentle rolling hills, the brooks, the meadows slightly powdered with snow, and filled her lungs with a deep breath of cold air. The coachman was right. A short walk would invigorate her and help her snap out of her doldrums.

Lu walked up along a small path when she reached a small picturesque cottage. In the summer, there would be roses climbing up the light grey stone walls. The thatched straw roof perched on top like a gardener's hat.

She gasped.

Here it stood, the cottage of her dreams. All that was missing was a dog, a cat, and several chickens. And as if that wasn't enough, a sign by the gate said: Rosebramble cottage.

For Sale.

Underneath, it said: Apply to Messrs Bromley & Brown for further information.

"I WISH I UNDERSTOOD WOMEN BETTER." Adrian Adey, Viscount St Addington, London's most notorious womaniser, said wearily.

Adam looked up from his missive with a thoughtful frown on his forehead. "It is no doubt a confounding situation." He shook his head. "However, I must say that a great part of the confusion lies on your doorstep. What on earth has got into you? I hardly recognise you anymore."

St Addington sighed. "What is so difficult to understand? She doesn't want to marry me. She never did. In fact, she holds me in contempt because of a certain incident that happened a long time ago. She has no reason to trust me, even if we did strike up a cordial sort of friendship. But it's been entirely epistolary. I confess I was reluctant, terrified, even, of the moment she made the connection."

Adam raised his eyebrows. "I don't seem to know this story. Tell me."

St Addington told him about the wager in the card room which Lady Ludmilla had overheard.

"I may have been directly responsible for Lady Ludmilla pulling out of her engagement with Matthew Fredericks," he admitted. "I helped ruin her prospects of marriage."

Adam pulled his quill thoughtfully through his fingers. "So you hid behind my nickname. I'd never have thought you so cowardly."

A flush crept up St Addington's cheeks. He rubbed his neck. "I thought that you, maybe, fulfilled more the image she may have expected. Which is why I asked you to meet her in front of the lending library instead of me. To test the waters, so to speak."

"Ah yes. And instead of Lady Ludmilla, Lady Jessica appeared." Now it was Adam's turn to blush.

"Spit it out, Cousin. Why the bashfulness?"

"It was a truly perplexing situation. I was more than happy to do you a favour, even step into your shoes for a while, for what harm is there to take a walk with a lady my cousin might fancy? You can't imagine how curious I was. The great rake finally showing serious preference for a woman! So, I went to that lending library and waited for Lady Ludmilla ... I was firmly determined to confess to her that I was Adam Adey, when instead of Lady Ludmilla, Lady Jessica showed up." He fixed his gaze on the letter he still held in his hands. "I was beyond surprised. So was she."

"Ah. I wonder why? Let me guess. She is the lady you have been corresponding with?"

Adam got up and took a turn about the room. "I was walking down Bond Street when I beheld a lady crossing the road, carrying a tall hat box in such a manner that she did not see the curricle that raced towards her. She stumbled and fell. There would've been a most tragic accident if I hadn't rushed to her and helped her across the street, just in the nick of time, for whoever drove those horses certainly would have been unable to stop."

"Well done. So that is how you met Lady Jessica. And you maintained a correspondence with her."

"Lady Jessica sent me such a prettily written card of Thank You that I could not help but reply in kind. We corresponded for a while. It was my intention to call on her, court her, even, but then she did not show up for our appointment. I fell ill and was unable to go to the balls and dinners you frequented. Then she suddenly stopped the correspondence, which, mind you, she had every right to do. But doubt befell me, especially when I heard that she was courted by all and sundry, and I assumed that maybe my attentions were not as welcome as I'd initially assumed. Until the day you asked me to stand in for you, and she seemed genuinely delighted to see me. At least, at first. After her sister joined us, she became rather quiet and withdrawn." He frowned.

St Addington grasped his head. "Adam. Good heavens. Never tell me when you proposed to Lady Ludmilla, your heart was, in fact, with Lady Jessica? Your honour as a gentleman is commendable. But what if she'd actually accepted your proposal?"

Adam looked at him unhappily. "I know. But I have grown fond of Lady Ludmilla, and we have become good friends. I don't think a union between us would have been that terrible. But I couldn't bear the notion of her being ruined. And I still don't understand why you, of all men, did not pursue the matter." He shook his head. "What are you going to do about it?"

What, indeed? It was a muddle. St Addington leaned back in his armchair tiredly. "I told you. I can't force her to marry me. Especially not Lu. I am, to be honest, at my wit's end."

Adam looked at him attentively. "My, my, Adrian. Who would've thought? You have finally lost your heart."

I have not, he was about to protest.

But then he knew that Adam was, of course, entirely right.

Adam jumped up. "Where is my hat? I need to go to Grosvenor Square and talk to Lady Jessica immediately. She looked so unhappy yesterday. I can't bear knowing that she is unhappy." The butler brought his coat and hat. He looked at St Addington. "What are you going to do?"

"I'm off to Covent Garden." He said curtly and took his hat.

Chapter Twenty-Seven

"Luuudmillaa!"

Lu dropped her quill. "Coming, Aunt!"

Goodness. What was the matter now? Aunt Mildred, far from having recovered from the bunions, dyspepsia, and the plague, now suffered from the ague, consumption, and scarlet fever. She'd consumed an entire crate of Dr Rothely's Elixir. At her wits' end, Lu consulted the doctor on what to do about her aunt. On the pretence of having to purchase more elixirs at the apothecary, she dropped by Dr Allan's house.

"Would you like my honest or diplomatic reply?" Dr Allan took off his glasses and looked at Lu with pity.

"The honest reply, if you please." Lu wrung her hands.

"Get her out of the house. Sunshine and fresh air. By all means, get her to take the waters, it certainly can't harm. Might as well take advantage of the baths since they are right in front of your doorstep after all. But, in all likelihood, nothing will bring about a cure since her ailments are not physical, but mental. The culprit behind it all is anxiety and depression. How long since her husband has passed?"

Lu hung her head. "Two years."

Dr Allan nodded. "You have to understand that she is still mourning."

"Of course." Lu nodded. "But what should I give her? She wants to try Snake Oil Liniment next."

"It's quack medicine. As long as she doesn't ingest it, it ought not harm her. Also keep the laudanum away from her."

He prescribed her valerian tea for the nerves, in addition to two hours in a mineral bath, followed by an hour sweating in bed.

He handed her the sheet. "If you manage to take her to the theatre, that would be the best medicine." He winked at her.

A rush of emotion flooded through her as she remembered the last time she was in the theatre.

No, she wouldn't go there, to the past. But the theatre ... it would be good for her, too, Lu thought as she opened the door to the apothecary. The bell jangled.

There were several ladies waiting in front of the counter as the apothecary hustled about, grinding powders, and filling them into little paper bags.

The ladies who were waiting fell silent when Lu entered.

"Good afternoon," Lu greeted them. They were neighbours, and while they were not closely acquainted, they were on greeting terms. However, it seemed, not today. Both ladies turned their backs to Lu.

They left without giving her as much as a glance.

What was that all about?

Lu obtained her valerian tea, the snake oil and another bottle of Dr Rothley's Elixir and walked home with slow, measured steps.

Was it just her imagination or did the women who approached her cross to the other side of the street?

She'd been too lost in her thoughts on the way to town.

But now there was no mistaking it.

People, especially women, were avoiding her.

As if she had the plague.

HER MIND IN INNER TURMOIL, Lu returned to her aunt's house. It was just a coincidence, she told herself. Maybe she was merely imagining things. She'd returned to Bath barely over a week ago. Surely gossip had not travelled so fast?

She'd never have thought it possible, but now that people avoided her, she veritably craved company.

Maybe that was what London had done to her. Forced by Ernestina into socialising, the impossible had happened: she'd gotten used to the dinners, picnics, breakfasts, suppers, visits to the libraries and galleries, the zoo and even Vauxhall, once. One event chased the other, for Aunt Ernestina had made sure their days were full.

Never in her entire life would Lu have thought that she'd begin to miss it all.

After several days inside Aunt Mildred's house, she'd become restless.

She had to get out. Doctor Allan had suggested the theatre.

She'd seen a playbill of *Hamlet* stuck to a wall. There would be a performance in the Theatre Royal.

Hamlet was just the thing. How could she persuade her ailing aunt to get up from her sofa for once and go to the theatre?

"The theatre! Are you out of your mind?" Her aunt stared at her, horrified.

"No, but I shall be if I have to remain walled in for much longer. It is most salubrious for one's mental health to entertain oneself once in a while."

"What nonsense. The best thing for the mind is rest and relaxation."

"Doctor Allan has specifically prescribed a more varied, active kind of lifestyle, which, he says, might be exactly the kind of thing for you to improve your health."

That caught her aunt's attention. "Doctor Allan, you say? I have been trying to get him to come for a visit, but he seems so occupied with other patients, all minor ailments mind you, compared to mine. When did you talk to him?"

"This afternoon. I asked him for a prescription."

She handed her aunt the paper.

Aunt Mildred perused it. "Hm. Valerian tea. Walks and a mineral bath? I must say I have not tried that yet."

"Maybe you should. We could go there tomorrow if you want. It isn't too far away, is it? And tonight is an excellent performance of *Hamlet*."

It took her the entire afternoon to convince Aunt Mildred to go to the theatre with her.

"I haven't been to the theatre in twenty years," she declared.

"Then it is about time, Aunt. Let us go. It will do us both some good."

Here was Ludmilla, who until recently, had to be coerced and bullied into attending any kind of social functions, convincing her aunt to go to the theatre.

"I don't know, Ludmilla. My feet ache most prodigiously."

Lu felt her temper flare. "Then I will have to go on my own," she snapped.

"Ludmilla! How can you! A lady never goes on her own." Mildred frowned in displeasure.

"See? Which is why you need to come with me. Put on a pretty dress and let's go. If you don't like it after ten minutes, we can always return home."

She now regretted that she'd left all her dresses in London. She ought to have at least taken along one. But what's done was done. She would have to make do with whatever she had in her wardrobe.

"Hm. I daresay London has thoroughly spoiled you. All this desire for entertainment. But I confess, I am curious now. I wonder whether the actors are as terrible as they used to be back in my time?"

"Let us go and find out."

"Very well then." She sighed deeply. "I see you will not relent unless I go with you."

Thus it came that Ludmilla and her aunt went to the theatre that night to watch *Hamlet*.

SHE RAN into him at the entrance of the theatre.

A man, clad in black evening clothes, like so many other men.

As Lu and her aunt walked past him, he pivoted and stared.

He looked vaguely familiar, but then, many individuals did, for Ludmilla had been introduced to many people in London. She had a terrible memory, and with the exception of St Addington's, could never recall any faces. Afraid of cutting a person she was supposed to know, she merely nodded at him and, taking her aunt's arm, continued her way up the stairs.

His piercing glance followed her. "Lady Ludmilla?"

Her head snapped around. That voice did sound familiar. She hadn't heard it in a very long time.

She turned.

The man broke into a smile. "It is you."

"Matthew?" It came out as a croak. It couldn't be. That was Matthew? Her handsome, dapper, tall Matthew in red uniform. Now a middle-aged, portly figure with receding hairline. Good heavens. What had happened to him?

"I would have recognised you anywhere." She couldn't exactly say the same about him. "How are you?" He took her hand and pumped it up and down.

"Matthew. What a surprise." Or shock, rather. How could a person change so much?

"Who is this, dear?" Aunt Mildred looked at him curiously.

"This is Captain Fredericks." Lu's voice was thick

with emotion. "Matthew, this is my aunt Lady Mildred Arbington."

Matthew bowed over her hand. "Lady Ludmilla and I knew each other in London...a while ago," he explained to Aunt Mildred.

"A while ago," Lu echoed. How long had it been, exactly? Ten years? More. How embarrassing to be running into him now. Matthew did not seem to feel the same, for he was beaming down at her.

"We had such a good time, back then, in London."

Did they?

"I recall all the parties and balls we attended," he told Aunt Mildred.

"Indeed?" She raised an eyebrow at Lu.

Lu squirmed uncomfortably but did not reply.

"We danced through the night."

"Not the entire night..." Lu put in.

"And spent the days walking in the parks."

"Did we?" Lu couldn't recall walking through the park with Matthew.

Well. Maybe they did. Hyde Park. Once.

"It was a good time, back then." He weighed his head back and forth.

Lu looked at him curiously. Her memory of the time wasn't as rosy, especially towards the end, even though she may have been somewhat in love with Matthew, back then. Oh, very well, she'd been besotted by him. But only at first. It was so easy to see the past through rosy-coloured lenses. She had to remember the time after-wards. When her heart had been broken. When she discovered he was nothing but a fortune-hunter, and she'd allowed herself to be deceived by him.

Why was he still beaming down at her as though he really had fond memories of their time together? It truly puzzled Lu.

"Well then, we ought to go..." Her aunt went ahead on the stairs. Lu nodded at Matthew and wanted to follow her aunt, but Matthew seized her hand.

He lowered his voice. "I know things ended on a less than positive note," he spoke so softly that Lu had to bend forward to catch what he was saying. "And I take responsibility for that entirely. I have often thought, when looking back over the years, not without some regret, that I owe you an apology. I may have led you to believe ... if my circumstances had been different..." he tangled himself up in his words. "That is, I just want you to know that whatever you may have thought, then, that contrary to my behaviour, my affections have always been sincere. I sometimes wish things had turned out differently."

Lu's mouth fell open. "But—"

He squeezed her hand hard and let go.

"There you are, Matthew. Where have you been? I have searched for you everywhere. Agnes, Mary, Papa is here." A tall, thin woman, with two girls in tow, stepped up to him and grabbed his arm. "Can't let this man out of your sight for one minute, and he will go and run off somewhere. Your cravat is crooked. I told you to let go of that valet of yours, he can't even tie a proper cravat. Let us go, Matthew. The play is about to start." The woman brushed Lu aside as she dragged her husband up the stairs.

Matthew threw Lu a last, wry look before he followed his wife.

"Are you coming, Ludmilla?" Her aunt raised an eyebrow. No doubt she'd watched the entire interlude from the top of the stairs.

Lu followed her into the box.

She had difficulty focusing on the play.

Had she just received an apology from Matthew, of all people? After all this time? Why on earth? And was it sincere?

Her emotions were turbulent.

The Lu she had been ten years ago, the naive girl she used to be, felt gratification. The Lu she was now... couldn't care less. It was like bandaging a wound that had healed a long time ago. Yet, a knot that had been buried deeply in her heart loosened. Lu clasped her hand in front of her chest. She blinked as tears rushed to her eyes.

She took a big breath.

If she found it so easy to forgive Matthew...What about St Addington? What was it about him that she found it so difficult to forgive?

Her eyes roamed the stage for a familiar figure, but, of course, he wasn't here. There was no Caliban on stage. None of the other actors was him.

St Addington was acting in London, not in Bath.

But she was sitting on edge the entire time, her eyes browsing through the audience, roaming the stage, looking, looking for a tall figure with a sarcastic, lopsided smile.

When recess came, she chid herself for being so foolish. The nervous excitement fled and left her feeling deflated.

In the pit, she saw Mrs Fredericks, Matthew's wife, talking rather loudly as she berated her husband over the choice of seats.

He was a hen-pecked husband.

Poor Matthew.

Lu felt sorry for him.

The past was the past, she told herself.

It was time to move on.

Chapter Twenty-Eight

Her aunt, far from wanting to leave after the first ten minutes, vowed she'd never been more entertained.

During recess, they stood in the refreshment room. Mildred even sipped some champagne and looked around with interest.

"It's been a while since I have been out and about in society, but one thing is clear. People never change. They delight in gossip now as much as ever," she told Lu with a disapproving sniff. Then she whispered, "You won't believe what Lady Spencer just told me while you were in the retiring room. The Duke of Macclesfield's daughter nearly eloped with that dandy Lord Stilton. I say nearly, because her father learned of it, thank the heavens, and prevented the elopement at the last moment."

Lu gasped.

"Shocking, isn't it? There is more to come. It turns out that that scoundrel Stilton never intended to marry the girl. He wanted to ruin her to get revenge on the father for some reason or other." Mildred waved a hand.

Lu clutched a fist to her chest. "But—but how did the father discover their intent to elope?"

Mildred took a sip of her champagne before answering. "It seems the father was tipped off anonymously."

"Anonymously?" she echoed.

"So they say. Isn't the entire story completely silly? I am only interested in the story because I knew Macclesfield. Once upon a time. My John and Macclesfield used to go hunting together." A wistful look crossed her face. "His daughter Cynthia is a pretty enough thing, but somewhat of a ninny."

It must have been St Addington. He'd overcome his cold indifference and done the right thing after all. She felt like her insides vibrated. A rush of emotions gripped her and left her breathless.

"Are you quite all right, Ludmilla?" Mildred asked. "There is an odd glow in your eyes, and your cheeks are quite red."

"I am just hot, Aunt. Nothing more." Lu fanned herself with the theatre programme.

It occurred to Lu that Mildred had not always been as she was now. Once upon a time, she must have been a young, lively debutante as much as any other. Indeed, it was as though the evening brought up memories, and she was slightly more animated than usual.

"I used to go to the theatre often when I was younger." Mildred fanned her peacock fan and smiled. "Ah, the memories! And funny how the faces changed so little over time. Look, there is Lady Wimple over there.

226

She has the exact same terrier look on her face as she did twenty years ago."

Mildred nodded at Lady Wimple, a buxom woman who stood with her three daughters several feet away.

Lady Wimple stared, froze, then turned her back towards them. Then she ushered her daughters, all debutantes, away.

"Did that woman just cut me? How excessively odd." Mildred frowned. She snapped her fan shut. "Maybe she hasn't recognised me. It has been a while since I was last in society. I will go over and greet her."

Lu caught her by her sleeve. "Maybe you should just leave her be." She had an inkling of what could be the matter. But her aunt was already in the process of descending upon them like a battleship.

"Clementia." Mildred tapped her fan on Lady Wimple's shoulder.

She made a small jump. "Mildred. Goodness me. I couldn't believe my eyes at first. It is you."

"Of course it is," Mildred said breezily. "I daresay it's been a while, but I would have recognised you anywhere."

"By all means." Lady Wimple seemed to struggle between being cordial and aloof. "I believe I haven't seen you since poor John died. It is as though you disappeared from the face of this earth."

"I have been ill on and off. I am better today, but the air in here is certainly giving me a migraine."

"A shocking squeeze," Lady Wimple agreed. "But nothing compared to London. We just returned from London, my daughters and I."

"So did my niece, Ludmilla." Ludmilla hovered in the background, wishing her aunt hadn't drawn attention to her.

"Indeed." Lady Wimple's voice turned chilly. "We heard *such* things. Shocking. I must say. Shocking!" She turned her back.

Mildred, who had no clue since Lu hadn't told her about what happened in London, frowned. She tapped Lady Wimple's shoulder again with her fan. "I see little has changed in London, if people still insist on being shocked about things."

"Yes, but not if they involve your, hm." Lady Wimple's eyes roved over to Ludmilla, who stared at the ceiling.

"Hm? What is that? Speak clearly, Clementia. My ears are not as good as they used to be. I just recovered from a most terrible ear infection."

"Your niece," she hissed.

"Ludmilla?" Mildred said that so loudly that some heads turned.

Ludmilla cringed.

"What about her? Come here, Ludmilla dear. Say hello to Lady Clementia Wimple. We used to be child-hood friends. Once upon a time."

Ludmilla took a big breath and curtsied. But Lady Wimple did not acknowledge her.

"Come, girls, we do not talk to The Fallen." Lady Wimple turned her back to her to usher her daughters away.

Mildred froze for one moment. "Well. I *must* say."

She rapped Lady Wimple's shoulder so hard it was more of a slap.

"Aunt!" Ludmilla hissed, half laughing, half crying.

"Pray unhand me," Lady Wimple said in the chilliest voice possible. "I do not converse with ruined women."

"Clementia, from what I remember, you never used to have the sharpest of minds, but what is this faradiddle you are pouring forth?"

"Don't tell me you don't know." Lady Wimple gasped in surprise.

"Very well: I do not know. Now tell me."

"I heard it myself from Lord Horton. And he is not one to tell Banbury tales. Your niece," Lady Wimple threw a wrathful glance at the shrinking Ludmilla. "Your niece had the audacity to kiss a rakehell. In the middle of the park. During Lady Somerset's winter picnic. For everyone to see."

"What prittle-prattle is this? Surely Ludmilla would never do such a thing."

"Why don't you ask her yourself?" Lady Wimple nodded at Lu.

They were already drawing attention as the people around them had fallen silent and gleefully followed the interchange.

Lu's face was burning scarlet.

"Ludmilla. Did you kiss a rakehell?" Her aunt's strident voice carried across the room.

Everyone heard her.

Hundreds of eyes were staring at her. The stuff of her nightmares. She saw the curious faces, the gleaming, gleeful eyes, so ready to judge a woman at the simplest transgression. They ignored the bell to return to the seats for the second act, for the drama that was unfolding here was so much more exciting than monologuing old Hamlet.

Lu could've cringed. She could've hung her head, taken her aunt by the arm, and dragged her away. She could've run and hidden in her aunt's house.

Something snapped in Lu. She was done with it. So done!

"Certainly, Aunt. What else is a hopeless spinster to do but kiss a rakehell? With her eyes open, too." Her voice rang out clearly and calmly, and more loudly than an actor's voice on stage. Everyone in the room heard her response.

There was shocked silence.

That was it, then. She would never be able to show her face in society again. Not that she found this overly tragic, but this happened at a rather inopportune moment, just when she was beginning to enjoy being more social.

But what was done was done.

Mildred gaped at her. Lu took her great aunt's arm and led her through the crowd, which parted in front of them like the Red Sea.

"Oh. How very well done!" a lady's voice exclaimed to her right. It belonged to a well-dressed, dainty woman with bouncing brown curls. She was laughing and clapping. "How utterly refreshing an answer. The wittiest retort I have heard in a long, long time. And you are entirely right, too. But forgive me. We haven't been introduced. I am the Duchess of Ashmore. I would very much enjoy making your acquaintance." She held out her hand to shake Lu's. "Do call on me in the coming days. Here is my card." She handed her a small, cream card with golden lettering. "I shall be expecting you." She nodded at Mildred. "Your companion as well."

"Th-thank you." Lu looked at the card, stunned.

The lady smiled at her amiably, took the arm of a tall gentleman, who nodded at her, and returned to their box.

A general murmur erupted, mixed with laughter and a scattering of applause. The applause increased. People nodded and smiled at her as she passed by.

Lu blinked.

She'd been elevated from the status of squashed spinster to that of eccentric wit within minutes.

And all because she dared to be truthful and finally speak her mind.

"THAT WAS one of the oddest theatre visits in my entire life," Mildred said in the carriage. "The Duchess of Ashmore! An invitation! Do you know that she is one of the most influential people in the entire Kingdom? Oh, how my heart is beating! Where are my pills?"

"I had no idea, Aunt." Lu was still dazed. "About the Duchess, I mean."

"I must say that cow Clementia hasn't changed one bit. As spiteful and hostile as always. She also grew fatter around the waist. And now, Ludmilla. Tell me exactly what you have been up to in London. From the very beginning. Including the story of that gentleman who accosted you earlier this evening. If I am not wrong, you have a former love swain there. He looked so melancholic."

Lu told her aunt the entire story. How she'd been nearly engaged to Matthew. How it had all broken apart. How she met St Addington, and how he'd kissed her. What she did not tell her was that she had been corresponding with Addy all this time.

Her aunt surprised her. She nodded. "My John was the same. A rake through and through. He chased one scandal after another. In the end, we eloped, you know."

What? Mildred had eloped with a rake?

Mildred smiled in reminiscence. "I met him at a masked ball in Vauxhall. It was the most romantic evening of my entire life. And even though I was already somewhat older, he took an instant liking to me. So, we eloped. We were happily married for twenty years before John left this earth. I daresay I never recovered from that." She dabbed at her eye with her handkerchief.

Who would've thought that Great Aunt Mildred had a romantic love life when she was younger? Underneath her hypochondria was a deep, deep sadness. Lu began to understand her aunt a little better.

She took her hand. "I am sorry you had to lose my uncle John so early. Naturally, you would still be sad about his passing. I am sorry...for having been so oblivious about this."

Mildred blew her nose. "Yes, well, it can't be helped. But you! It looks like life is about to get somewhat more interesting here."

When they entered their house, Mildred told the

maid, "I may not need the elixir tonight." There was more of a spring in her step when she climbed the stairs.

Lu's words travelled fast. How fast, she learned in the coming days, when a letter from Jessica arrived.

Ludmilla!!!!

The most incredible thing has happened! The entire ton is in upheaval because of you. You are famous! We received word that Humphreys is displaying a Cruikshank caricature of you and St Addington. Apparently, it is selling so well they can't keep up with printing! Aunt Ernestina immediately dragged me to St.James's Street, and indeed, a crowd of people was gathered in front of the window of the print shop to view the displays. It is a very scandalous print of a garish dandy, draped helplessly over the arms of a horridly dressed spinster, as she tries to kiss him with puckered lips, saying "What else is a hopeless spinster to do but kiss a rakehell?"

There are no names, but everyone knows who it is meant to be. How utterly shocking and witty and coura-geous of you if you did, indeed, say this! I am somewhat upset that they made such a horrid figure out of you, but I do have to admit it is quite funny!

Aunt nearly fainted on the street, then marched into the shop to buy one print, only to find they had all been sold out. Aunt was certain this was the nail to your coffin, and that your reputation is hopelessly destroyed, etc., etc. BUT—people are so strange! They seem to like it!

Including the Prince Regent! Yes, you read that right. They say he slapped his knee, laughing, and asked who that lady was and that he would very much like to meet her! Word got out, and now everyone is visiting us to inquire whether you indeed said those infamous words in the theatre. Aunt doesn't know what to do with all those invitations! People are fairly scrambling all over themselves to be the first to host you. Has Prinny contacted you yet? You must tell me the moment he does!

I am laughing as I am writing this. Dearest Lu. Do write quickly and tell me immediately: Did you indeed say this?

Your sister,
Jessica

Lu CHOKED on her breakfast bun as she read the letter and broke out in a coughing fit.

"Oh dear, oh dear, oh dear!" She did not know whether to laugh or cry.

A Cruikshank cartoon? Of herself and St Addington? Exhibited in the middle of St. James?

Now she really had become the laughingstock of the *ton*.

And all because she'd kissed a rake.

And now the Prince Regent wanted to get to know her personally!

If this had happened several months earlier, Lu would have taken a shovel, dug a huge hole in her aunt's garden, and buried herself in a fit of humiliation. Now, she felt unholy amusement well up in her. People were

234

strange, indeed, to first condemn and censor, and then to celebrate a spinster like her.

How odd that instead of this making her even more of a pariah, it seemed to do the opposite. People recognised her on the street, but, unlike before, when they turned their backs on her, they pulled their hats and greeted her. One could make neither heads nor tails of people's behaviour. A shame that the prints were sold out, for she'd have loved to see what it looked like.

Like Jessica had described in her letter, the invitations came pouring in. Only this morning, they received three invitations to an afternoon tea, one invitation to a breakfast, two concerts and a ball.

"I hardly know any of these people," Lu told Mildred at breakfast one morning, overwhelmed.

"Take a few and turn down the rest is my advice. You are now in a position to pick and choose the kind of company you want to keep." Mildred, when she wasn't forevermore focused on her many ailments, turned out to be rather good company, and Lu found herself developing more and more of a liking to her. She had not given up her pills and elixirs entirely, but at least she no longer objected to Lu pulling the curtains aside and allowing the daylight to flood the rooms.

Life, Lu found, was becoming more bearable.

Chapter Twenty-Nine

THAT MORNING, LU HAD SOME IMPORTANT BUSINESS to conduct. She had a meeting with Messrs Bromely & Brown to discuss the possibility of buying the cottage she had seen on her trip to Bath.

"The property is indeed for sale." Mr Bromley steepled his fat fingers together on the table. "However, we will only consider serious applicants." He was a bald, rotund gentleman who felt important as he sat behind his mahogany desk. His entire demeanour seemed to imply that he was not taking Lu very seriously.

"I am serious," Lu told him.

He lifted an eyebrow. "My dear Miss—"

"The name is Lady Ludmilla Windmere."

"Oh. Indeed. My lady." He sat up straight.

"I would very much like to buy this cottage." Lu had savings a-plenty, in addition to the inheritance she had received from her father. She could buy an entire mansion if she wanted.

This, too, finally dawned on Mr Bromley. A gleam of interest entered his eyes. "If you would have a seat, my lady." He got up and pulled out a chair for her.

Lu sat.

THE COTTAGE WAS HERS.

Of course, she would still require her lawyer to handle the necessary papers, signing of contracts, and transfer of funds. But ultimately, she'd come to an agreement with Mr Bromley that she had first claim on the cottage. Once the paperwork was done, she could move in.

She walked down Milsom Street with a bouncing step. Passing the apothecary, she decided to make a quick stop to pick up some liniment rub for her aunt.

In the shop were several ladies who nodded at her genially.

"Lady Ludmilla. How do you do. Have you received my invitation to tomorrow's musicale?"

Lu probably had, but she could not, for the life of her, recall who the woman was, so she merely nodded and smiled at her. "It will be a pleasure to see you there."

The women nodded back and walked on.

"I heard that St Addington has finally been caught," one lady told the other. She lowered her voice. "I wonder whether she knows?"

Lu's hand froze on the door handle.

"No! That is almost unbelievable. The man has eluded women since I can remember."

"Nonetheless, it is true. My brother saw him in a

jewellery shop on Bond Street the other day." The woman bent over and whispered loudly so that Lu could hear it, too. "He bought a wedding ring."

"Now, that is a delicious piece of gossip if there ever was one. Do you know who it is for?"

"They say, in all likelihood, it is for Miss Peddleton. Apparently, he danced twice with her that evening." She clucked her tongue.

"A nobody. Really? That is almost tragic. When he could have any woman he chooses."

Lu had had enough.

Surely, surely this was just a rumour. If life had taught her anything, it was that she should never listen to rumours. But the pain that had pierced through her heart just now was difficult to ignore.

She left the shop without even buying anything.

THAT NIGHT, Lu couldn't sleep.

She was hot, then cold, then hot again, but it had nothing to do with the down blanket that covered her.

She got up, opened the window, and let the cool night breeze brush over her skin.

Then she went over to her desk, took out a fresh sheet of paper, and wrote a letter to Addy. Not St Addington, not Adam Adey, but her own, very own Addy. The friend who did not exist. The Addy whom she'd imagined ever since she began writing letters to him.

She imagined him sitting by the fireplace, petting his dog Macbeth, as he read the letter. He would chuckle over certain phrases, smile over others, and then pick up his quill and write back.

DEAR ADDY, *my dear friend,*

Oh, how I miss talking to you. For our letters have always been conversations, haven't they?

For the first time, I wish you were here so we could really talk.

I am so confused.

I miss you terribly.

I feel that there is no person on earth who understands me as much as you do.

Yet, I feel this confusing longing for someone who you may know very well.

It is St Addington.

He is a terrible rake. And a terrible flirt. And I should cut him out of my mind immediately. Yet, I can't stop thinking about him. And here I am, in the middle of the night, writing this letter like a love-sick schoolgirl.

Oh, Addy, I fear the worst has happened.

I fear I have fallen in love with him.

But he is to marry someone else.

What to do?

What to do?

I wish you were here to advise your distraught friend,

Lu

SHE FOLDED IT, in smaller and smaller squares, pressed it to her heart. Of course, she would never send it.

But now that it was out, now that she had written it all down, she felt oddly at peace.

How ridiculous it all was. It definitely wasn't love.

It was just infatuation.

Like with Matthew.

Exactly like Matthew.

Chapter Thirty

For a while, Lu's and Mildred's days grew to be quite busy. They attended dinners and musicales and, to their surprise, enjoyed it more than they thought they would.

Lu packed her cap back into the drawer again and began wearing dresses in colours other than brown.

Then she received a letter.

Dearest Lu,

I have such news!

I am engaged to be married to Adam Adey! He came the other day with a gigantic bouquet of roses and proposed to me in the most romantic way. Oh, Lu! I am so happy. And now it is time for me to confess. I never did tell you that it was he who helped me across the road when I had that near-accident. We corresponded for a while after that, but then I had such doubts. I thought myself in love at first, but then I wasn't sure. Aunt Ernestina insisted all the time that I marry a titled gentleman, and I feared she would not find Adam acceptable since he had no title. So, I kept his identity a secret, even from you. Poor Adam! He thought I did not reciprocate his feelings. I thought it best to forget him. Then things got so confusing. I laboured under a misapprehension for the longest time, when I thought that your beau, and the person you were corresponding with, was Adam! Especially when he turned up in front of the circulating library, when you asked me to meet him in your stead.

Oh, I was so surprised and distressed! Even so, I did not tell you who Adam was. I did not, under any circumstances, want to come between you two if Adam was the man who had claimed your heart. For my Lu also deserves some happiness in this world. I admit I could not help but be in deep anguish when he proposed marriage to you that awful afternoon. It was then that I understood that I really did love him.

But everything turned out all right in the end, did it not?

Adam proposed so prettily, and now I will be the happiest woman alive.

Please tell me you will return to London for the wedding, for we want to get married in St. James's in two months' time. Aunt Ernestina is quite happy, even though rather confused with the development of things. I do believe she is still somewhat cross at you for having turned down St Addington, but I daresay she will get over it eventually, especially now that you are so famous.

With much Love,

Your happy sister Jessica

Jessica and Adam Adey!

A small smile flitted over Lu's face. Of course. Why hadn't she seen it earlier? She'd been so absorbed with her own problems that she'd overlooked the obvious signs. Poor Jessica, how she must have suffered. Her little sister, who she had always thought spoiled, had a generous heart and was capable of great sacrifice.

"Oh, Jessica," Lu whispered. "I am so happy for you and Adam."

Lu found another letter waiting for her one afternoon, after she returned from a walk. The handwriting was very familiar. Her heart flipped, then pounded away at a ridiculous pace.

She tore the missive open with trembling hands and perused it.

Lady Ludmilla.

> *You are such a goose. Let's talk this out.*
> *I will call on you tomorrow.*
> *Your obedient servant,*
> *Addy.*

A hand crawled up to her throat. Did her eyes deceive her? She read the letter again.

He clearly said he was going to call on her tomorrow.
But how?
But why?

It clearly read as a response to ... Sweet, merciful heavens, it couldn't be!

Had she accidentally sent him the letter she'd written in the middle of the night? A cold fear gripped her heart.

"Hicks!" she bellowed.

The butler appeared, startled that she'd raised her voice. It must be the first time in his career of butlerhood at Great Aunt Mildred's house that someone had raised her voice. "My lady?"

"Did you mail a letter the other day? One that I'd left on my desk?"

"Yes, my lady. It was addressed to Bruton Street, London. Like so many others before, I assumed you'd want it to go out on the next mail coach."

Lu could barely bring out the words. "That can't be. Didn't I throw it away?"

"No, my lady."

"I actually put the address on it?"

"Indeed, my lady. It was also sealed and ready to go."

Heat flooded through Lu's face. "But—I did not! I crumpled it up ..." her voice trailed away. Actually, she hadn't. She'd folded it up. And in her distraction, maybe she even scribbled the address on it, with the intention of crumpling up the paper afterwards. Maybe she hadn't. Quite possibly, Hicks may have seen it, thought it was ready to be posted—

"Oh no," she whispered. "Oh no, no, no, no!"

She could barely remember what she'd done. She may have very well forgotten to burn the letter. And Hicks, faithful butler that he was, had seen it, and posted it.

"My lady? Are you well?"

She stared at Hicks. "Sometimes, Hicks, I wish you weren't such a good butler."

He blinked and clearly did not know how to take this.

Lu waved him away. "Never mind, never mind."

What was she to do?

Now Addy had read her letter, and he was coming all the way from London "to talk it out".

She walked up and down in her room with agitation, her heart hammering in her chest. What did he want to talk out? It sounded ominous. There was nothing to talk about! What should she tell him? That she'd made a terrible mistake?

That she didn't really know what she'd been writing? That she was very fond of her long-term friend and pen pal? That she really hadn't meant him at all?

Lu broke out in a sweat.

She ought to write a response that it was entirely unnecessary for him to come, he should please stay where he was, namely in London—when it hit her that he would never receive her letter.

It was likely that he was in Bath already.

What to do?

Lu grabbed her head with both hands and groaned loudly.

"Ludmilla! Are you in pain?" Mildred came out of the drawing room, concern written over her face. "You look terribly pale." She pushed Lu into a chair.

"Yes. I am in shock over my own foolishness," Lu informed her aunt.

"I am not certain what that means, but I do know that

it can't be any good. Do you need hartshorn salt? Dr Rothely's Elixir? The liniment?"

"All three, Aunt, please. In addition to a good dose of valerian tea. My nerves!"

Mildred patted her arm. "There, there. Go and lie down. I will make sure the maid draws the curtains shut."

Lu allowed herself to be led to her bed, certain that this was the worst day of her life.

Chapter Thirty-One

After a sleepless night, Lu stayed by the window the entire morning, peeking between the curtains to see whether she could catch a glimpse of a particular gentleman walking up to the house.

She knew, of course, that "morning call" did not literally mean morning, and that the caller she expected was likely to show up in the afternoon.

Nonetheless, she could not help herself. She stayed by the window all morning, chewing on her fingernails, only to completely miss the moment when he must have walked up to the house.

It must have happened while the maid asked her whether she would like to have a tray brought up to her room, and she'd turned away from the window to talk to her.

"No, thank you, Mary." She wasn't hungry at all. Even if she were, she would not be able to swallow because her throat had formed itself into a knot.

She suddenly heard baritone voices in the hallway, as the butler ushered him into the drawing room.

Lu jumped, paled, and wrung her hands.

She thought of pretending to be ill. Maybe there was no need to pretend, even, for she already felt quite weak and hot, and her heart hammered irregularly.

She could instruct Hicks to tell him that she wasn't at home.

The door opened, and Hicks entered. "A certain Mister 'Addy' is here to see you. He refused to give me his full name, and he had no calling card. It is most irregular. Should I throw him out?"

For a wild moment, Lu considered it. It was cowardly. She shook her head. "I will be down in a moment."

WHEN SHE SAW him stand by the window, looking out, her nervousness fled, and she felt quite cross.

"I knew it was you."

The gentleman by the window turned.

"Lady Ludmilla."

"I hate the name."

"Understandable."

"And yours?"

He shrugged. "Adrian."

"Adrian Edward Adey, the Viscount St Addington." Lu plopped down on the settee, suddenly weary. Her knees had finally given way. Her breath came out ragged.

"The other way around. Edward Adrian. But since

250

my cousin is called Edward as well, the name Adrian stuck."

"Addy."

"A childhood remnant."

Lu shook her head. "But Adam is Addy."

"People mispronounce our family name all the time. Addy-Adey. People confuse us as well. This time, I thought it was rather convenient."

"You wretch! You let me believe all this time that Adam was you."

"I feared your wrath if you discovered it was me." He looked contrite.

"But I did. At first. I made the correct connection. But then I got confused, and you encouraged the confusion."

He smiled at her charmingly. A dimple appeared. Lu looked at him darkly and folded her arms across her chest.

"You look terribly cross. I am afraid what I am about to say will make you even crosser." He shifted from one leg to the other and rubbed his neck.

"I came to Bath a month after our correspondence started." He looked apologetic. "We'd exchanged three letters, maybe. I walked by your house once or twice, thinking about calling. Thinking of knocking and introducing myself. Then I saw you come out of the house. Mind you, I did not properly see you as you were hiding behind your umbrella. I got cold feet and changed my mind at the last moment."

He'd done exactly the same as she had. In London. Lu furrowed her brow. "I don't understand. Why all this charade? Why not just tell me who you were? Did you enjoy playing with me?" She sounded bitter.

"No, Lu. Is that what you think? It would never occur to me to play with you." His eyes, for once not icy, burned with determination.

"Then why?"

"Because—" He jumped up and took a turn about the room. "I did not think you would have handled it well had you known who I was. Because of what happened with Matthew."

He may have a point.

"I wanted us to get to know each other naturally. But then, in the meantime, you made the connection about when you'd last seen me—in that card room. At our next meeting, it was obvious that you did remember, and that you clearly despised me. I don't blame you. My behaviour back then was despicable, to say the least. At the same time, you were uncertain about whether I really was your correspondent Addy. I must confess; I was too much of a coward to admit it. Besides, Adam was doing a fantastic job at being Addy. And then, the longer we continued this, somehow the more difficult it became to break out of it."

"But at that first meeting," Lu said slowly, "when you walked up to me in the circulating library, why did you not wait outside at the bench yourself?"

"Because I've grown to know you rather well, and I knew my Lu would do exactly that." He took a step forward. "Hide in the library to see who I was. If you'd seen me waiting by the bench, you'd never have come forward."

She blushed at him saying "My Lu". What he said was true. He really did know her well. He'd known her all along.

"And the second time, you wheedled Adam into pretending he was you." Her voice sounded condemning.

"Hm. Yes. Evidently, I remained a coward. But then —I might say the same thing about you when you sent Jessica instead. Adam, too, played along because he was so delighted that his rake of a cousin finally fell for a woman."

Lu blushed fiercely. "What I don't understand is why you kept up the charade. It would have been the moment to call me out, but you decided not to do it, and I felt —uncertain."

"The truth is that you despised St Addington so much, he could just remain his usual cad self, but I feared, truly feared that your feelings would turn to hatred if you made the connection that I was Addy. Lu. Can you ever forgive me?" The regret in his eyes was honest. "I was terrified of losing you. Yes, I know I could've just not allowed it to unfold to begin with. That day when I saw you waiting by the lamp post in front of my house? Walking by you, pretending I did not know who you were was the most difficult thing I ever did in my entire life. Well, nearly the most difficult one." He swallowed. "What I am about to do is by far the most difficult." He rubbed his hands and walked up and down in front of her, stopped, resumed pacing.

He took a few steps about the room, stopped once more, and looked at her. "What I actually came here to do was—dash it all, why does this have to be so difficult?"

He broke off and took out a letter from his pocket. "Did you mean what you wrote in here?"

Lu blanched. "That letter was an accident—I never intended to send it. I didn't even know I sent it until Hicks told me!" She reached for the letter, but he snatched it out of her reach.

He grinned. "You most certainly did send it. Thank the heavens."

Lu groaned.

Adrian went up to her and knelt in front of her. "Tell me you meant it." His eyes burned into hers. "Tell me."

She covered her face with her hands and shook her head. He pulled them away.

"Tell me you meant it."

"I am so sorry. I am terribly, awfully afraid..."

His face fell.

Lu took a big breath. "This is the most humiliating moment in my life. But I am afraid I meant every single word in that awful letter. I will burn it immediately if you'll let me, and you can just ignore I ever wrote it, and you can continue as though nothing has ever happened."

She fished for the letter once more, but he held it out of her reach.

A light shone in his eyes.

"Lu. Ludmilla." She opened her mouth to add on another string of reasons of why she made a mistake. He interrupted her. "My Lu."

He kissed her quite thoroughly.

And Lu completely forgot what she was going to say.

A wonderful while later, she sat on his lap with disorderly hair and stars in her eyes.

"I saw that caricature." His mouth twitched with amusement. "I woke up one morning, and all of London insisted on talking to me about it. Including the Prince Regent. He insists on meeting you, by the by. Adam laughed so much, he nearly rolled on the floor. You are wonderful, Lu, do you know? It was the most marvellous thing to say. I will get you a copy of the print for a wedding present. We will frame it and hang it on the wall."

"That is a prime idea, Addy." She clutched at his neckcloth, deliriously happy. "Oh!" she pulled back as she remembered something. "You did finally do something about Stilton and Lady Vanheal. You were the one who warned the father anonymously, did you not?"

"Hm. I might have."

"After protesting you would never get involved in another man's affairs." Lu grinned.

"My conscience left me no peace. Besides, I thought it wouldn't hurt if it helped get me back into your good graces."

"Another thing, my lord." She frowned again. "I nearly forgot. They say you are supposed to be marrying that terrible Miss Peddleton. You were seen buying an engagement ring for her."

He pulled out a little box and handed it to her. "This, maybe? This was meant to be for you. I don't know anything about Miss Peddleton."

"And why were you courting Jessica? To make me jealous? If this was your motivation, it grieves me to say that you have succeeded."

"Were you indeed? Jealous?" He grinned and tugged

at a strand of her hair that had come loose. "I was temporarily unhinged and convinced that Adam might be the perfect man for you. That you might be happier with him. So, I thought to get Jessica out of his way, seeing she was a distraction to him. Rather infernal of me, I know."

"You wanted to matchmake me and Adam?" Lu blinked at him.

"Hm." He nibbled at her ear.

"But. Why?"

"I thought you two were the perfect pair. Adam seemed very taken with you, and I believed he developed feelings for you. At that time, I did not know he was in love with Jessica. I thought, since you were better off with him than with me, I decided to help things along. Utterly maggot-headed of me, I know."

"Very."

She opened the box and gasped. Inside was a lovely ring with a single diamond stone. It was lovely and elegant in its simplicity.

She lifted her head to smile at him, and he promptly took advantage of it by kissing her once more. "I should inform you that I intend to live in the countryside in a cottage with several chickens. I have already bought the house," she told him after a while.

"I don't care where you decide to live as long as you allow me to live with you." He thought. "Maybe, once in a while, I will have to go to the theatre in Bath or London to keep up with my acting. What do you say? We join Adam and Jessica in St. James's for a double wedding?"

"I would love that beyond anything," she sighed.

"One thing I am still wondering about. When, in the end, did you finally make the connection that Addy really is me?"

"Easy. You gave yourself away."

"How so?"

"Sugar plums. You ate up the entire plate."

"I did, didn't I?" He slapped the side of his head.

Lu nestled her head against his chest. "A happily ever after thanks to a plate of sugar plums."

Also by Sofi Laporte

The Wishing Well Series:

Lucy and the Duke of Secrets

Arabella and the Reluctant Duke

Birdie and the Beastly Duke

Penelope and the Wicked Duke

A Christmas Regency Novella:

A Mistletoe Promise

Wishing Well Seminary Series:

Miss Hilversham and the Pesky Duke

Merry Spinsters, Charming Rogues:

Lady Ludmilla's Accidental Letter

About the Author

Sofi was born in Vienna, grew up in Seoul, studied Comparative Literature in Maryland, U.S.A., and lived in Quito with her Ecuadorian husband. When not writing, she likes to scramble about the countryside exploring medieval castle ruins, which she blogs about here. She currently lives with her husband, 3 trilingual children, a sassy cat and a cheeky dog in Europe.

Get in touch and visit Sofi at her Website, on Facebook or Instagram!

amazon.com/Sofi-Laporte/e/B07N1K8H6C

facebook.com/sofilaporteauthor

instagram.com/sofilaporteauthor

twitter.com/Sofi_Laporte

bookbub.com/profile/sofi-laporte

Made in United States
North Haven, CT
30 July 2022

22055605R00161